'12

PLE END ON TO NEXT
BRA 3 MONTHS

RID USE
EAS ON
BAI STON
SHE NORTH
MO NORTH
PA EAD
BR ETON
POILPARK
MI ON
BA MULLOCH
SPRINGBURN
ROYSTON
DENNISTOUN

Was it so obvious that she was in love with Blake?

She hoped not.

He'd already made it clear that he didn't want her to keep expressing her thanks. So how would he react if he discovered her feelings went a lot deeper than that? Since the day they'd kissed he'd never touched her, and she didn't know why.

She wished she knew. But maybe tonight the answer would present itself. Just the two of them alone in the cosy cottage.

POLICE SURGEONS

Heart-racing romance—
Heart-stopping drama—
Medicine on the beat!

Working side by side—
and sometimes hand in hand—
dedicated medical professionals join forces
with the police service for the very best
in emotional excitement!

From domestic disturbance
to emergency room drama, working to
prove innocence or guilt, and
finding passion and emotion along the way.

THE POLICE SURGEON'S RESCUE

BY
ABIGAIL GORDON

MILLS & BOON®

*First published in Great Britain 2004
Large Print edition 2004
Harlequin Mills & Boon Limited,
Eton House, 18-24 Paradise Road,
Richmond, Surrey TW9 1SR*

© Abigail Gordon 2004

ISBN 0 263 18170 7

*Set in Times Roman 16½ on 18 pt.
17-1004-52115*

*Printed and bound in Great Britain
by Antony Rowe Ltd, Chippenham, Wiltshire*

CHAPTER ONE

So this is it, Helena thought as the taxi pulled away and she was left standing at the bottom of the drive surrounded by her luggage. 'Home sweet home'.

It looked decent enough, the small detached house in a suburban cul-de-sac, but it wasn't the place where she'd been brought up. That had been in a town much farther north than this, in a pleasant house on a road not far from the noise and bustle of the city.

Looking around her, she wondered what she was going to do in a place like this. She'd like to bet the folks around here were all in bed each night before ten. Maybe her dad was beginning to feel his age and that was why he'd moved, but he could at least have consulted her first. He'd known she wasn't going to be away for ever.

The door opened and he was there, smiling at her. Putting to one side her feeling of grievance, she ran up the drive and into his arms.

He looked older and thinner, Helena thought as they carried her bags inside. He'd lost the robust jollity that had kept them going after they'd lost her mother, and even though she'd only just set foot in the place she had to ask, 'Why did you move house, Dad? This is miles away from all the places I know. Why didn't you tell me what you were planning? I couldn't believe it when I got your letter. I know the old house was a bit big for the two of us after Mum died but...'

There was no smile on his face now. It was more sombre than she'd ever seen it.

'I'm going to put the kettle on, Helena,' he said, 'and when we've had a cup of tea I've got a story to tell you that will explain why I've done what I have. I'm afraid that you're going to think this is a very poor homecoming.'

'Fine,' she told him, feeling better now that she'd got it off her chest and having no inkling that 'fine' was the last word she would think of to describe the situation once she'd heard what he had to say.

Later, much later, as she lay in a strange bedroom, exhausted but sleepless after the long flight, she was trying to take in what she'd been told and amongst a jumble of emotions the one uppermost was fear.

As Blake Pemberton looked down on the body of the man lying on the smooth green turf of the golf course his eyes widened beneath raised brows. He'd seen plenty of dead bodies since he'd started working with the police in a medical capacity and the causes of death had varied. Natural causes, accidental and in some instances the victim had died in suspicious circumstances.

But it wasn't any of those factors that were causing surprise. For the first time ever he'd been called out to examine the body of someone he knew. It was the elderly man who'd moved into the house next door who was gazing upwards with sightless eyes.

'Somebody walking their dog found him, not long ago,' one of the policemen who'd been summoned to the scene told him, 'and when we radioed back to the station they said to ask you to come out to examine him before we moved him. What do you think, Doctor? There's no obvious signs of injury.'

Blake had got over his surprise and was examining the body of his neighbour with swift expertise. Noting the froth on blue lips, the grimace of pain on the waxen features. The body was still faintly warm but there was no pulse or heartbeat. Getting to his feet, he told the constable, 'I would think he suffered a massive heart attack. Even if help had been at hand I don't think it would have made any difference.'

As the policeman nodded his agreement Blake told him, 'You don't have to worry about his identity. He's my next-door neighbour. Only moved in recently and was living on his own until yesterday when he was expecting his daughter home from Australia. So there's sorrow for someone.

'I don't know if she's actually arrived but if you like I'll go and break the news to her, and if she's not there I'll put a note through the door asking her to contact me.'

'Sure,' the other man agreed. 'I'll leave it in your capable hands and we'll get the poor fellow to the mortuary.'

As he drove back home Blake wasn't looking forward to passing on such sad tidings to the man's unsuspecting daughter, but it wouldn't be the first time he'd had to break that kind of news to a member of the public, far from it. The good, the bad and the unthinkable were all part of the day-to-day routine of the GP.

It was a quarter to eight in the morning and thankfully it was Sunday, otherwise he would be having to dash off to the surgery once the deed was done. The man must have gone for an early morning stroll and it had turned out to be his last.

Helena awoke to the ringing of the doorbell and for a moment she lay there, bewildered, wondering where she was, then it all came back. As the bell rang once more she still didn't move waiting for her father to answer it, but it rang again and this time she swung herself out of bed and padded to the window.

The caller had given up. He was walking down the drive with a purposeful step, a tall, dark-haired man, broad-shouldered, trim-hipped, dressed in jeans and a sweatshirt.

She opened the window to call to him and then thought better of it. After what her father had told her the previous night the less they had to do with strangers the better, and she shrank back into the shadows.

But he'd heard the window catch being lifted. He stopped and turned and even though he couldn't see her he called up, 'Could you come down to the front door, please? I need to speak to you urgently.'

There didn't seem any point in cowering out of sight if he knew she was there, so showing herself she leaned forward and said, 'I'm listening.'

He frowned.

'I don't want to tell all the neighbourhood. It's about your father.'

'Yes. I'll bet it is!' she cried. 'If you don't clear off immediately I'm going to call the police.'

'I *am* from the police,' he said patiently, with the feeling that this was going to be even worse than he'd imagined, 'and I'm also your next-door neighbour. My name is Blake Pemberton. Will you, please, come downstairs? I have some grave news concerning your father.'

'Hold on!' Helena cried.

If it was a hoax her father would be in the dining room, having his breakfast, but if that was the case, why hadn't he answered the door?

He wasn't there. But a scribbled note was. It said, 'Gone for a stroll along the golf links. Will cook you breakfast when I get back.'

As she stood with the note in her hand Helena could see the man's shadow through the glass of the front door, and with dread in her heart she went to open it. Not knowing if it was the right thing to do, but with the certainty that if something had happened to her dad she had to know.

Her first thought as the door swung back was that he didn't look like a thug. There was nothing shifty about the level gaze meeting hers and he was making no move to come any nearer.

'I realise from your manner that you are wary of me for some reason,' he was saying, 'but I do assure you I mean you no harm. It was true what I said. I *am* with the police. I'm a doctor, working with them. They were called to the golf links a short time ago as the body of a man had been found by a passer-by and they got in touch with me in my position as police surgeon.

'Sadly it was too late for me to help him. There was nothing I could do. But I did recognise the man as your father and offered to come to tell you what had happened. I am so very sorry to be the bearer of such bad news.'

If her face hadn't been so transfixed with horror she would have been beautiful, he thought. High cheekbones, a sweetly curving mouth and green eyes beneath a tangled russet mop.

Her pyjamas weren't the last word in glamour, soft cotton with no frills or flounces, but those were details scarcely registering as she croaked, 'Oh, no! So they got to him after all. How could they?'

As Blake eyed her questioningly she began to crumple and he caught her as she fell. As she wept in his arms he asked above the crown of her head, 'What's your name?'

'Helena,' she sobbed. 'Helena Harris.'

'So tell me, Helena,' he coaxed gently, 'what did you mean by what you just said?'

He felt a shudder go through her and silently thanked the providence that had sent him to her in such a moment of distress.

'My dad was the only witness to a shooting on a garage forecourt some months ago in the town where we lived. He testified in court and after that received threats. So the police took him into the witness protection programme and moved him out here.

'He wrote and told me he'd moved but didn't explain why until I came home yesterday. I've been in Australia, nursing, for the last twelve months. But it was all a waste of time, wasn't it?' she sobbed. 'They found him in spite of everything.'

'No,' he said softly. 'It wasn't like that, Helena. Your father died from natural causes. He had a massive heart attack out there on the golf course and there was no one about to help him, Though I doubt it would have made any difference if there had been. So, you see, there is nothing to fear. If you'd like to get dressed I'll drive you to where they've taken him.'

'He wasn't murdered, then,' she whispered.

'No. There were no signs of injury on his body. It's my job as police surgeon to look out for that sort of thing, and there was nothing. But there was evidence of a massive cardiac arrest.'

'I'm so sorry that I was so dubious of you when you came, but you can understand why, can't you?' she asked, moving out of his arms as if she'd suddenly realised where she was.

She looked sad and very vulnerable and yet there was a sort of quiet dignity about her as she stood before him in the sensible pyjamas.

'So go and get dressed,' he suggested again, 'and while you're gone I'm going to make you a cup of hot sweet tea.'

Helena nodded mutely and padded back up the stairs. When she'd gone he put the kettle on and then stood deep in thought. His expression was grim. The girl and her father had been traumatised because the man had done his duty as an honest citizen, and who was to say that the heart attack hadn't been a direct result of the position he'd found himself in?

There'd been no mention of her having a mother. He hoped that she did have someone to turn to, and as she sipped the tea that he'd made Blake asked carefully, 'Do you have anyone to help you through this sad time? Brothers, sisters or any other relative you can rely on?'

Helena shook her head. 'No. I'm afraid not. I'm an only child and both my parents were the same, so I've no aunts, uncles or cousins.'

She was calm now but pinched-looking and drained of all colour. When she'd drunk the tea she got to her feet.

'Will you, please, take me to where my dad is?' she asked.

'Yes, of course. My car is the black Volvo outside the house next door. Here's the key. Go and settle yourself inside and if you'll give me a door key I'll lock up behind us.'

Helena looked around her and shuddered again.

'Yes, please. This place feels spooky to me after what Dad told me last night.'

He couldn't leave her in that house tonight, Blake was thinking as they drove to the hospital mortuary. She was having a horrendous homecoming. Yet what was the alternative? Would she be willing to sleep in his spare room?

They hardly knew each other. She might think spending the night in the house of a stranger even more nerve-stretching than the thought of who might be lurking. When he got back he would impress upon the police to make public the fact that the witness in the recent trial was dead, so that if the friends of the convicted man had been trying to find James Harris, they would now give up.

*   *   *

Helena clung to Blake's hand when they were shown her father's body, but she managed to hold back the tears when a doctor came to inform her that there would have to be a post-mortem.

On the way back Blake made up his mind what he was going to do, and when they stopped at the front of their two houses he said, 'Would you like to use my spare room tonight? You've had a dreadful shock and I would like to keep an eye on you.'

Surprised green eyes met his as he posed the question.

'That's very kind of you, Dr Pemberton. Are you sure I wouldn't be in the way? Do you have family?'

He shook his head. 'No. There's just me. I did have a family once, but they aren't around any more.'

'Oh. I see.'

She didn't, of course. Didn't see at all, but what else was there to say if he wasn't going to explain further? And it looked as if he wasn't.

'In that case, I would very much like to stay. I should have got a better grip on things by tomorrow and thank you for your kindness. I couldn't have got through the ordeal at the mortuary without you.'

'I'm only too happy to have been of help,' he told her, 'and if I make us a belated breakfast, do you think you could manage to eat something?'

'I don't think so. Please, see to yourself and while you're doing that I'll go next door and do some unpacking. My things are still in the cases from when I arrived last night.' She halted in the doorway and with the unease back in her eyes said, 'Will you be around for the rest of the day?'

'Yes, I will,' he told her firmly, thinking that this young woman's needs were of more importance than the couple of rounds of golf he'd promised himself later in the day. Also, did he want to see the links again so soon after what he'd been faced with on his earlier visit?

When Helena came back that evening she was very pale but composed. 'I've made the funeral arrangements,' she told him. 'There will be just myself.' After a moment's hesitation she added, 'Unless you would care to come as moral support.'

Blake didn't answer immediately and she said quickly, 'I'm sorry. I shouldn't have asked. I've already put on your good nature enough as it is.'

'Of course I'll support you,' he told her. 'I was just wondering when you'd arranged it for as I'm senior partner in a group practice not far from here and if it is in surgery hours I'll have to find a replacement.'

'It's at half past one next Monday,' she informed him, 'which gives them time to conduct a post-mortem.'

'Good. That will be between surgeries. One of the other partners can do my house calls.'

'Thanks, Dr Pemberton. I'll be really grateful for your company and when it's over I suppose the best thing would be for me to book a return ticket to Australia.'

'Were you intending going back?'

'No. My contract was up. But there's nothing to keep me here now. I have no job and when the witness protection people come to want the house back I'll have no home, and in any case I wouldn't want to be in there on my own.'

'What kind of nursing were you doing?' he asked with a degree of interest that surprised him.

'I did six months in obstetrics and six months in paediatrics. I fancied a change and off I went. I knew nothing about the court case until I got back last night and I was horrified when Dad told me that he'd been in such danger...and maybe still was.

'He hadn't been a bit keen for me to come home, but I'd thought it was because I'd let him see how upset I was over him selling our old house. I didn't know that it was my safety he was concerned about.'

And that makes two of us, Blake thought grimly. The police had better get their act together and get any possible revenge attacks sidetracked now that her father was dead.

This beautiful sorrowing woman was getting to him as no one had for a long time. She was arousing all the protective instincts that had lain dormant ever since he'd lost his wife and son.

At ten o'clock Helena said, 'Would you mind if I go to bed, Dr Pemberton? It's been a terrible day and I'm exhausted.'

'Of course I don't mind,' he told her. 'The bed is made up. Shall I give you something to help you sleep? A mild sedative maybe?'

Helena shook her head. 'No. I'll try to manage without.'

She was moving towards the staircase and he said, 'Just one thing before you go, Helena.'

'Yes?'

'The name is Blake. Forget the Dr Pemberton.'

There was weariness in her smile as she told him, 'I'll remember that. Goodnight…Blake.'

When she'd gone he sat unmoving, but if his body was still his mind wasn't. All sorts of thoughts were going round in it. The kind of thoughts that less than twenty-four hours ago would never have had cause to surface.

His reverie was interrupted by the doorbell and as he got to his feet he could see a car belonging to one of the partners in the practice parked at the bottom of the drive.

He sighed. Maxine Fielding was a good doctor. She was also husband-hunting and Blake had a feeling that she saw him as prey. The seas would run dry before he succumbed to her, he kept telling himself, but he was loth to create an embarrassing situation at the practice unless he was forced to.

When he opened the door to her it was clear that in spite of the hour it was a social call, and before he could nip it in the bud she'd seated herself and was telling him that she was gasping for a gin and tonic.

He obliged, with eyes upward raised and ears pinned back for any sounds from above, but all was still until Helena's voice called from the top of the stairs, 'I think I will have the sleeping tablet if you don't mind...Blake.'

Maxine was on her feet faster than the speed of light and, peering up the staircase at the person responsible for the unexpected interruption, she said tightly, 'And who might that be?'

'A guest,' he told her calmly, and to Helena. 'I'll be up with it right away, Helena.'

'So?' Maxine said when he came back down.

'Helena is the daughter of my next-door neighbour who died suddenly today. The police called me out when his body was found and I had the unenviable task of breaking the news to her that her father was dead. She is very distraught, needless to say, and I felt that she shouldn't be alone tonight. Does that satisfy you, Maxine?'

'I suppose so,' she said tartly, 'but I'm not going to stay and chat with someone listening upstairs.'

'You flatter yourself if you think Helena will be interested in anything we might have to say after the sort of day she's had.'

'Nevertheless I'm going,' she said, 'and don't forget we have a practice meeting arranged for after morning surgery tomorrow.'

'I'm not likely to forget,' he told her drily. 'I *was* the one who arranged it.'

There were three partners at the practice—himself, Maxine, who had come highly recommended from a practice that he'd since discovered had been glad to see her go, and Darren Scott, a young, recently qualified GP.

Darren and Maxine didn't get on too well as she was always criticising him instead of offering encouragement, and Blake was left to keep the peace. The rest of the staff were a hard-working, contented lot and for most of the time there was harmony.

He'd started working for the police twelve months previously and from the beginning had pledged himself to help those of the public, whether innocent or guilty, who found themselves in a cell because they were suspected of breaking the law.

His duty was to protect them from harming themselves or anyone else, and if a prisoner was taken ill to be there to see that they received proper treatment. There would be no deaths in the cells if he could help it.

His relations with the police were good. They knew they could rely on him to turn up when sent for and that his findings would be meticulously passed on to them.

*   *   *

When Blake had brought her the sedative Helena said apologetically, 'I'm so sorry, I didn't know you had a visitor.'

He smiled.

'Think nothing of it. Maxine Fielding is one of my partners from the practice. She won't be staying long and as soon as she's gone I shall be turning in myself. Remember, Helena, if you need anything in the night you have only to call.'

'Yes, I know,' she said gratefully and turned her face into the pillow, wishing that she didn't look so ghastly and that she wasn't wearing the shapeless pyjamas.

Helena cried out in the night and Blake went to her. As he soothed her back to sleep he saw the sedative was on the bedside table. She was a nurse, he thought, and would know that no matter what she took to help her sleep she would awake to desolation in the morning. Clawing her way out of the same kind of black hole that he'd crawled out of every morning for a long time after Anna and young Jason had been killed in a car crash on the school run on a bright spring morning three years ago.

He still had his dark days but time *did* heal. It wasn't just a platitude that was trotted out to help the grieving. Gradually the pain eased and if one was lucky only the happy memories remained.

Hopefully that was how it would be for his unexpected visitor, only in her case there'd been fear to cope with, too.

When he awoke in the morning Helena had gone. She'd found an empty envelope and had written on the back of it, 'Have gone home. There is much to sort out. Thank you for last night, Blake. I hope I didn't disturb you too much as I know you have a busy day ahead. Best regards, Helena.'

As she'd been writing the note her face had been burning. She'd known that he'd held her some time during the night, but she'd been too exhausted and traumatised for it to register properly, and in the light of day she hadn't been able to believe that she'd let her night-mares be soothed away by a man she'd only known a matter of hours. Yet it hadn't felt like that. It had been as if she'd known him always.

For the rest of the day she tried to keep busy. A police sergeant and a young constable called in the middle of the morning and told her that they were making sure that the newspapers printed an account of her father's death. That should finally wrap up his connection with the Kelsall case, they told her, and surprised her by saying that it was at Dr Pemberton's suggestion.

As she tried to force a sandwich down at midday Helena began to wonder about his visitor of the night before. The aggressive-looking blonde with the cold grey eyes had glared up at her as if she'd been about to steal the silver, and she wondered if they were a couple. She hoped not. Blake Pemberton deserved better than that. Much better.

She was humbly grateful that he'd agreed to attend her father's funeral with her. For the moment she couldn't think any further than that. But once it was over it would be decision time, and of one thing she was certain—she wasn't staying in this house.

Maybe she could find something in nursing over here with accommodation thrown in. The authorities in the UK were always saying there was a shortage of nurses. It might be the time to test the water.

The practice meeting in the late morning was going smoothly enough, with the manager announcing that they were meeting their budget and Blake's two partners for once not bickering. But it took a downward turn when a letter from one of the two practice nurses was read out, asking that she be permitted to leave at the end of the following week. No reason was given but most of the staff were aware that she'd just found herself a new man, a Welshman, and wanted to move to Wales to be with him.

'Shall I advertise?' the practice manager asked, and Blake shook his head.

'Let's leave it for a few days,' he suggested. 'I might know of a replacement. If nothing comes of it we'll advertise then.'

It would be one way of keeping an eye on Helena, he was thinking. Purely from a protective point of view...of course. Not for any other reason. She'd felt so fine-boned and vulnerable both times he'd held her close that he knew he would be on edge if she was out of his sight in the weeks to come.

He was worried because she had no one to turn to but himself. Yet wasn't he in a similar position? But he had a lot more going for him. He had the practice, his job with the police and his own home. In other words, plenty to occupy him...

As they left the meeting to go out on their calls Blake was waylaid by Maxine.

'Well,' she said. 'Has she gone?'

'If you mean Helena, yes,' he told her coolly. 'I've left it to her to decide if she wants to come back tonight.'

She was eyeing him dubiously.

'You'll have people talking.'

He laughed and her face tightened.

'Maybe it's time I gave them something to talk about.'

'*I* could help with that,' she said skittishly.

'I was joking, Maxine,' he told her. 'Anna would be a hard act to follow and I don't see suitable replacements on every street corner.'

He could tell that had gone down like a lead balloon but she didn't get a chance to reply as a patient she'd seen earlier was hovering. Relieved to be away from her, Blake set off on his rounds with the intention of making Helena's house his first stop.

'Why didn't you stay for breakfast?' he asked when she opened the door to him.

She looked awful. There were dark smudges beneath eyes that were red-rimmed with weeping and her face was even paler than the day before.

'How much sleep did you get?' he asked, as the doctor in him took over.

'Some,' she replied, with her face warming again at the memory of how he'd held her in his arms and comforted her in the dark hours of the night. To cover her confusion she said, 'I'd like to invite you for a meal to make up for all you've done for me, but I haven't got around to doing any food shopping, and as

Dad lived rather frugally there isn't much in the fridge.'

'I wouldn't dream of letting you cook for me,' he said immediately. 'You're in no fit state. But there's no reason why we can't eat out. I'll take you for a meal. It will be one way of making sure you're managing to get some food down.'

His glance was taking in the uncluttered worktops and a sink bare of used pots. 'Unless you're a very tidy person I would guess that you've had nothing so far.'

Was he overdoing the caring neighbour bit? he wondered. She'd turned away and was staring through the window. Maybe she was finding him too overpowering.

Yet she was saying, 'I'd like that. To dine out. It will help to take my mind off everything for a little while.'

He was smiling and Helena thought that this attractive stranger really was doing his best to be supportive, but there was still one thing that Blake Pemberton couldn't make right for her, even though he'd done his best.

She pointed to the early edition of the evening paper lying on the kitchen table, and as his gaze transferred to it she said, 'On the inside page.'

Blake picked it up and turned to where she'd said and his eyes narrowed as they focused on a short piece at the top of the page. The police had done as he'd suggested. It said that James Harris, the main witness in a recent gangland trial, had died of natural causes the previous day. That was all, but hopefully it would be sufficient.

It was the kind of scenario that he'd been on the edge of in some of the incidents where the police had asked for his assistance in recent months. Especially in some of the more rundown parts of the city. So it wasn't all that new to him.

But to this innocent woman who'd come back from Australia, expecting life to be as it had been before, what she'd been met with must seem like a nightmare. Not only was she having to cope with losing her father, she'd been touched by the seamier side of life in the process.

'I'm still wondering if I should go back to Australia to get away from all this,' she said, breaking into his thoughts.

'Yes, but do you want to?'

She'd thought she did, but now she wasn't sure. If she went back she would never see Blake Pemberton again. Their meeting would end up as just ships that had passed in the night and she didn't want that. She liked him. Liked everything about him. If that woman from last night *was* special, it didn't matter. She would be happy to have him as just a friend.

CHAPTER TWO

'I DON'T know whether I want to go back or not,' Helena said into the silence that had followed Blake's question. 'There was nothing to keep me there and now there's nothing to keep me here.'

It wasn't the moment to mention that there was a vacancy at the practice, but he would bring it up while they were eating tonight, he decided. It would give Helena the chance to be thinking about it while she waited for the funeral to take place.

He had another suggestion that he was going to tag onto it and felt that it might influence whatever decision she came to, but that could wait until that evening, too.

And so he sidetracked the issue by saying, 'There'll be time to worry about that when you've laid your father to rest. And with regard to tonight, you are welcome to use my spare room again if you don't want to be on your own in this place.

'Or, if you want, I'll come and sleep on the sofa here. But, Helena, do remember that no one, apart from those involved in the witness protection scheme, knows where your father had been moved to. There are no details of where he was living in the piece in the paper, so you should be quite safe here until you decide what to do.'

She nodded, turning away from him again as she did so, and he hoped she wasn't thinking that he was implying she was making too much of the situation she found herself in.

'Yes. I know, Blake,' she said flatly. 'I'm not usually so reliant on others. It's just that I can't seem to gather my wits after finding out from my father what's been happening while I've been away, and then you bringing me the news of his death so soon afterwards. Of course I'll be all right here. I've intruded into your life enough as it is.'

He was wishing that he hadn't said anything now. In trying to reassure her he'd put her on the defensive. Made Helena feel she was letting everything get out of proportion. He was going to have to tread more carefully. The last thing he wanted was to alienate her at such a time.

'You haven't done anything of the kind,' he assured her and changing the subject, he went on, 'I'll pick you up at seven o'clock if that's all right. There's a small restaurant not far from here where I dine when I want something special. The food is good and so is the service.'

Blake found he was holding his breath. He sensed that she'd gone into her shell. Was she going to say she'd changed her mind?

'Yes, all right,' she agreed listlessly. 'I'll see if I can find something decent to wear.'

She was dressed in old jeans, a sloppy coarse-knit jumper and had taken her hair off her face with a rubber band. It would be nice to see her in something else, he thought. Yet he knew that beneath the nondescript outfit were slim hips, firm breasts and skin that had been soft and fragrant to the touch when he'd held her close.

Helena Harris had been propelled into his life and he didn't want her to disappear from it as suddenly as she had come. She was the first woman he'd really looked at in a long time, but he was pretty sure that she saw him as if through a fog. In her present state, he didn't think it would register with her if he were seven foot tall and wore a leopardskin.

When he'd gone on his rounds Helena went to the mirror and looked at herself. Her face was drained of colour. It hadn't seen make-up since she'd left Australia. Her hair was unkempt, her clothes begging to be sent to a rummage sale. Blake must be dreading what she was going to look like when he took her out to dine later.

It was as if she'd had a personality transplant. The level, uncomplicated attitude that she applied to life in general had been replaced with a zombie-like trance, and who could blame her? She'd spoken briefly with her father on the night of her arrival. It hadn't been pleasant, and the next thing she'd known he was gone for ever.

But into the middle of her nightmare had come a stranger, a man who had taken her into his care and supported her through some of the worst hours of her life. She owed it to him to make herself presentable, and with the first lifting of her spirits since she'd arrived back in England she set about repairing the ravages.

When Helena opened the door to him that night Blake's eyes widened. Her dress of clinging silk was the same colour as her eyes and brought out the glints in her russet hair. Carefully applied make-up gave colour to a face that was still ashen from shock and grief, and if the thought of food made her feel physically sick her smile didn't give any inkling of it to the man who was putting his own affairs to one side on her behalf.

She'd had a couple of half-hearted relationships before she'd gone to Australia, both of them with hospital staff that she'd worked with, and had gone out with a husky Australian for a couple of months while she'd been over there, but none of them had made her heart beat as fast as it was now.

Blake had style and presence as well as a sort of rugged attractiveness, and she wondered what he'd meant when he'd said that his family weren't around any more. Was he divorced and his wife had taken the children with her? He didn't look like the sort of man who would neglect his family commitments.

He was returning her smile.

'I feel I must have got the wrong house,' he said teasingly. 'I'm looking for Helena Harris and you don't bear any resemblance to her.'

'The answer to that is simple,' she told him. 'I spent some time in front of the mirror and what I saw was not a pretty sight.'

He took her hand, holding onto it for a fleeting second, and then tucked her arm in his.

'Let's go and eat,' he said.

The moment they walked into the restaurant the proprietor, a fair-haired man in his forties, came forward to greet them with outstretched hand.

'Dr Pemberton,' he said warmly. 'Good to see you...and the lady. How are things with you?'

'Fine, Robert,' he replied. 'How's that brother of yours?'

The man shrugged his shoulders.

'All right as far as I know. I try to keep tabs on Michael, but it isn't easy with this place to run.'

He was showing them to a table and Blake said, 'I would think that last episode will have made him think twice about a repeat.'

'I hope so, but he still drinks too much,' the other man said, and handed them the menu.

'Are you wondering what all that was about?' he asked Helena when they'd ordered.

She nodded.

'Robert's younger brother was arrested on a drink-driving charge and put in the cells for the night. The police sent for me in the early hours because he'd been complaining of severe stomach pain, but when I got there the discomfort seemed to have gone and they were wishing they hadn't been panicked into calling me out. But, of course, they can't take any chances. When a prisoner dies in a cell all hell is let loose.

'I wouldn't go without examining him. They're not the only ones who don't take chances. There was something about him that worried me and to cut a long story short I found signs of a perforated appendix.

'As we both know, appendicitis can be fatal and the time of greatest danger is when the agonising pain suddenly disappears. If he'd been left all night he might have died as the police would have taken no heed of his drunken mumblings, the pain having gone.'

'And so you saved his life.'

He smiled. 'Only partly. The hospital had something to do with it, too. He was operated on immediately.'

'He and his family must have been grateful for your presence in the cell. I can see why his brother was so welcoming when you appeared.'

'Yes, *we've* become firm friends, but Michael, the guy who had the appendicitis, is still drinking too much for his own good and everyone else's.'

'You must get a lot of job satisfaction from your police work.'

'Yes. I do,' he agreed. 'Just the same as when I've been able to bring a patient back to good health. And with regards to the practice, how would you like to work for us?'

She stared at him in amazement. 'In what capacity?'

'Practice nurse, of course. We employ two, but one of them wants to leave in a hurry. As early as next week, in fact. If you are interested, I have another proposition to put to you.'

Still taken aback, she asked, 'And what's that?'

'I have a small house that I rent out not far from the surgery. It was my wife's before we were married. It's vacant at the moment. If you took the job you might want to consider living there instead of where you are now. '

'I've never worked in general practice,' she explained. 'I've always been hospital-based.'

'Does that matter?'

He wasn't going to tell her that he'd offered her the position because he wanted her near him. He wasn't sure why, but he did. Maybe it was because she'd been left high and dry after her father's death and he was concerned for her. Or were his motives more selfish than that? He didn't want to get bogged down in self-analysis.

He could imagine Maxine's reaction if Helena took the job. Fortunately he had the main say and if she didn't like it, too bad.

'I'd like to think about it if you don't mind,' Helena was saying. 'I feel that you've already done enough for me.'

Suddenly he was the senior partner rather than her good Samaritan. 'You would be expected to cope with a heavy workload and would get no special concessions from me.'

'I wouldn't expect any!' she exclaimed. 'I'm used to being treated on my own merits. What about the woman who was at your house last night? Did you say she was connected with the practice?'

'Yes, that was Maxine Fielding. She and Darren Scott are the other two partners. By all means think about the offer. I just felt that both suggestions might solve your problems for the time being.'

So he had no thought of it being on a more permanent basis, she told herself. No need to feel flattered that Blake was keen to employ her. Once again he was merely trying to be supportive at a time when she needed someone. He was anticipating that once she'd got herself sorted she would move on.

Yet what had she expected? They'd only known each other a couple of days. It was incredible that he was making her such an offer in so short a time. The suggestions he'd made were like a lifeline in her present situation and even if they hadn't been, there was a feeling of rightness about them that she couldn't ignore.

'Tell me about yourself,' he said as they ate a leisurely meal. 'How long have you been in nursing?'

'Ever since I left school. My mother was a nurse and I always wanted to be the same.'

'So you find it fulfilling.'

She was smiling and he thought how different she looked. She ought to do it more often, but he reminded himself that since they'd met she'd had very little to smile about.

'Yes, I do. Fulfilling...and tiring,' she told him, adding on a sudden impulse that she knew she might have cause to regret, 'You already know quite a bit about me, but I know nothing about you, except that you're a GP who is also involved in police work. You said that your family weren't around. Dare I ask why?'

She watched his expression change and wished she'd contained her curiosity. It was as if a cloud had settled on his face, but his voice was pleasant enough as he told her, 'You can ask, but I'm not sure whether I want to answer. If I do it will bring painful memories into a pleasant evening.'

'I'm sorry,' she said contritely. 'I presume something awful must have happened.'

'It did,' he agreed heavily. 'My wife, Anna, and our seven-year-old son, Jason, were killed in a car crash three years ago.'

'Oh, you poor man!' she said softly. 'You must think I'm making a big thing out of what has happened to me. No way does it compare with that.'

'I don't think anything of the kind,' he told her. 'I'm only too sorry that you came home to what you did, but I think a change of subject is called for.'

Helena nodded her agreement and said, 'So tell me about the practice.'

He launched into an account of a visit he'd made that afternoon to elderly twin sisters who were always ill simultaneously with the same complaint, and how, garrulous and hyperactive, they vied for his attention.

She was laughing as he described their antics and Blake thought that it was incredible that this green-eyed woman was fancy-free. Or was she? She hadn't said so. There might be someone in Australia anxiously awaiting her return.

Though if that were the case, she wouldn't be hesitating about going back, would she? And if she'd left some guy behind when she'd gone out there, he would have been the one she'd turned to rather than himself.

'If you'll excuse me for asking, how old are you, Helena?' he asked.

'I'm twenty-five.'

'And commitments?'

It was one way of asking if she was unattached, though it misfired somewhat.

'You know that I haven't. I've already told you I was an only child.'

'I was referring to relationships.'

'Oh, I see. Would it matter if I was in one?'

'No. Of course not,' he said smoothly. 'But again it's the sort of thing you might be asked about by the other two partners.'

'But not by you?'

'No. Not by me. I'm offering you the job because of what's happened.'

'Because you're sorry for me, you mean?'

'Yes. Partly. And also because you came back to a raw deal. I admire your father for what he did. There are lots of folk who won't risk life and limb in the cause of justice, but he did. Thankfully no one got to him, which is not surprising as the witness protection service allows for no margin of error. So your father died the way the rest of us hope to go...naturally.'

He wasn't offering the job because he was attracted to her, then, she thought wryly. She'd been a fool to think he might be. Blake Pemberton, senior partner, police surgeon... and childless widower...must have them queueing up for the chance to take his dead wife's place.

Blake had allayed her fears about going back to the house but Helena was in no hurry to return. As they lingered over coffee at the end of the meal he said, 'So are you happy to go back to the house? You don't have to if you don't want to.'

'No. I'm fine,' she told him. 'I'm not afraid any more. And, Blake, I *will* take the job at the practice if you're sure you want me. And I'll rent the house, too. You've solved all my problems for me.'

She meant it, but couldn't help feeling that with the sorting of one lot of problems others might appear, focused around a one-sided attraction.

'Good,' he said. 'I'm glad you've decided to accept. Maybe you could call at the practice some time tomorrow to meet the rest of the staff and have a chat with the practice manager. Would you be able to start the day after the funeral? That's when the nurse employed at present wants to leave.'

'I'd be glad to,' she told him. 'As then, more than ever, I will need to be occupied.'

When he pulled up outside their two houses Helena said, 'Thanks for your time…and the meal, Blake. I can't help but feel that I'm being something of a nuisance.'

He smiled and in the shadowed interior of the car she experienced the same feeling of familiarity that she'd felt earlier. Theirs was a very new relationship but it didn't feel like it. She felt safe in this man's company. Maybe it was because he knew so much about her in such a short space of time.

'The only time you're likely to be a nuisance is if you keep insisting that you are one,' he was saying easily. 'If you feel I'm being too intrusive, you have only to say so. Otherwise, I've promised myself that until you're over this awful thing that has happened to you, I'm going to be around. And if you're coming to work at the practice, we're likely to be in each other's company for some time to come.'

Why did her heart lift at the thought of that? she wondered. She had only to observe him and the answer was there. Blake Pemberton made every other man she'd met seem insignificant, but there was nothing to say that she was having the same effect on him. If what he'd just said was correct, she was more in the waifs-and-strays category than that of the desirable woman.

When he'd seen her safely inside the house, Blake said, 'Shall we say midday tomorrow for you to meet the team at the Priory Practice?'

'Yes,' she agreed, adding as the memory of cold grey eyes came to mind, 'Are you sure they won't object to me joining them sideways, so to speak?'

'My partners respect my judgement and will be only too relieved that we're not going to be without a practice nurse for any length of time,' he assured her. 'The only problem would be if you weren't up to the job, and somehow I don't see that particular difficulty arising. You have references, of course?'

'Yes. Though the ones from Australia might take some time to reach you. Unless you ask that they email them.'

'No problem. We'll sort that out. Lock up after I've gone. I can assure you again that you *are* safe here…and once you move into that house of mine you'll feel even safer. It's available as soon as you feel like making the transfer.'

'Tomorrow?' she suggested, wasting no time in taking him up on the offer.

'Yes, if you like…tomorrow. I had it contract-cleaned after the last tenant, so it's ready for you to move into any time.' He was looking around him. 'It's furnished, by the way. Do I take it that the stuff in this place goes with the house?'

'Yes. My father said that he'd put our furniture in storage, so I might as well leave it there.'

She couldn't believe it was happening. Earlier in the day she hadn't been able to see where she was going to go from here, and now she had a job and a new place to live. Would she ever be out of his debt?

But it seemed that Blake was still out to make her realise that he wasn't expecting it to be permanent as he said, 'Yes, leave it where it is. Then whenever you decide to leave us it will be there waiting.'

So it *was* only the waif-and-stray treatment she was getting, Helena thought wryly. Within his pledge to protect the living while in police care and help bring justice for those who had met their ends through foul play, he was doing his best for another lost sheep...herself. And she wasn't sure that was how she wanted it to be. He was seeing her at her worst. Lost, weepy and floundering.

When this was over she would have to show him that there was another side to her. That she was her own person, independent, resilient and a good nurse. Suddenly it was vital that Blake should have a good opinion of her, and he was offering her the chance to do something towards that end by taking her on at the practice.

With spirits lifting at the thought, she watched him go down the drive. When he reached his own front door he turned and waved, and as she waved back Helena knew she wanted him to be more than just someone who had befriended her in a time of trouble.

*   *   *

When Blake announced at the beginning of surgery the next morning that he'd found a replacement for the practice nurse who was leaving, Darren said, 'Great stuff. What's she like? Nice-looking, I hope.'

Blake didn't reply. His glance was on Maxine and he knew what was coming next.

'And where have you so conveniently found a nurse at such short notice?' she wanted to know.

'You've already met her briefly,' he said with bland pleasantness. 'The woman who has just lost her father, Helena Harris. You saw her the other night when you called.' Before she could interrupt he went on, 'She's been nursing in Australia for the last twelve months and had no sooner come home than her father died.'

'Then it was obviously her lucky day when she met you, Blake,' Maxine said frostily. 'Don't you think you're rather overdoing the good-neighbour bit? First of all you have her staying with you and then you're suggesting bringing her into the practice.'

'None of us know when we may need a friend,' he told her, without raising his voice. 'It might happen to you one day, Maxine.'

'That could be a bit tricky,' Darren said, and found her cold gaze transferred to himself.

'Helena is coming in to meet everyone at the end of morning surgery, so you'll both be able to have a chat with her then. In the meantime, we have patients waiting to be seen,' Blake said, ignoring the ever-present sparring between the two.

He'd anticipated a cool reception when Maxine heard of his plans and that Darren would be his usual flippant self. But he wasn't all that bothered about either of their reactions. If he discovered he'd made a mistake by offering Helena a job at the practice, he would take the blame.

He had other concerns regarding her and the main one was that after going out of his way to befriend her, he'd sent out conflicting signals the night before by inferring that he wasn't expecting anything permanent to come of their acquaintance when all the time she was never out of his thoughts.

Was he so out of touch with the chemistry between the sexes that he felt the need to put up fences when it appeared from an unexpected source? he'd asked himself during a restless night.

As someone who never did anything by halves, his love for Anna had been deep and strong. In the three years since her death he'd had no yearnings towards any other woman. Certainly not Maxine.

Then out of the blue had come a young nurse with beautiful green eyes and russet hair. *She* was getting to him as no other woman had, and what was he doing? Encouraging the relationship one moment and the next stepping back from it.

But the folks in the waiting room had their problems, too, and he was about to be confronted by them.

Amongst them was a middle-aged woman suffering from blackouts for no apparent reason. Being the kind of patient loth to bring her concerns into the open, she'd been slow to seek a consultation, but after having hurt herself quite badly from the last fall she'd been persuaded to seek help.

There were no signs of high blood pressure. It was rather low if anything. An examination of her eyes indicated no problems there. She wasn't suffering from headaches. In every way she seemed to be in good health, though obviously she wasn't. Blackouts were not something to be ignored and he referred her to the neurology department at the hospital.

A woman in her twenties followed her into his consulting room. She had digestive problems that he'd felt were cause for alarm and he'd sent her to hospital for tests. The results were now back.

They weren't exactly life-threatening but they were not good. Dark eyes in a thin face were watching him apprehensively from the other side of the desk and, always reluctant to put the blight on the lives of the young, he gave her a sympathetic smile.

'It is what I thought it might be, Samantha,' he told her. 'Coeliac disease or gluten enteropathy as it's sometimes known. The type of biopsy they gave you at the hospital shows that you have a gluten problem. A failure to absorb the nutrients from wheat, rye, and other cereals.

'All the unpleasant things that have been happening to you are the result of the illness. The anaemia, skin problems, poor bowel functioning and the rest should gradually disappear once you're on a gluten-free diet.

'With all other foods you should have no problem, but it will be essential to keep off wheat products. Other tests will follow to make sure that the diet is working, but I think that very soon you're going to feel much better.'

'So I'm not going to die?' she breathed, with the beginning of a smile.

'No, you're not,' he said gently. 'You've had a worrying and distressing time but we're going to put you on the right track. The nurse will give you diet sheets and will answer any questions you might have regarding food.'

She was getting to her feet and as he observed her pallor and weight loss Blake thought, poor girl. She was so frail. Hopefully by the next time he saw her she might have filled out a little and have some colour in her cheeks.

As Helena hesitated beside Reception at twelve o'clock, a cool voice said from behind her, 'And you are?'

When she swung round the woman who'd called at Blake's house the other night was observing her as if she were something best seen under a microscope.

'I'm Helena Harris,' she said levelly. 'Dr Pemberton is expecting me. He's offered me the position of practice nurse and invited me to come in to meet the staff.'

'Really. Well, he must have forgotten as Dr Pemberton is not on the premises.'

'Has he been called out perhaps?' Helena asked in the same even tone.

'I'm sure I don't know. You'll have to come back some other time,' she was told.

'Yes. I can do that,' she agreed equably. 'Time is something that I have in abundance at the moment.'

'I think there's been a mistake, Dr Fielding,' another voice said at that moment, and Helena saw a fair-haired man, younger than Blake, eyeing her appreciatively from the doorway.

'Dr Pemberton received a call from the police station just as surgery was finishing,' he said with a winning smile that showed a lot of white teeth. 'He left a message to say that he would be back as soon as possible and for you to make yourself at home while you're waiting. My name is Darren Scott. I'm the junior partner here and I volunteered to look after you until he gets back.'

'And in the meantime everything goes to pot, does it?' the unwelcoming Maxine said.

'Surely, not with *you* around, Dr Fielding,' he said, and Helena knew what Blake had meant when he'd said that these two weren't the best of friends.

'There is no need for you to look after me,' she told him. 'As Dr Fielding has suggested, I can come back another time.'

She was beginning to wish she hadn't come at all. The last thing she'd expected was that Blake wouldn't be there. Obviously it had been unavoidable, but five minutes with Maxine

Fielding had damped her enthusiasm somewhat.

'Dr Pemberton wouldn't like that,' Darren
insisted. 'He was most emphatic that you were
made welcome. If you'd like to come this way
I'll introduce you to Jane Benyon, the other
practice nurse. She's been here for years and
will be only too happy to show you the ropes.
She's the person you'll be working with most.
Then there's the practice manager, Beverley,
who keeps us all in order and tells us off if we
prescribe drugs that are too expensive.'

This was better, Helena thought as she met
the rest of the staff. Jane Benyon looked as if
she was climbing up to retiring age. She had
a kind smile and twinkly blue eyes. Beverley
Martin, in her late forties, was a smart type in
a suit, with dark hair in a short stylish cut and
a brisk manner that indicated a person who got
things done. The three receptionists were all
friendly and by the time they'd done the
rounds Maxine's hostility was fading.

When the call had come through from the police Blake had given an exasperated sigh. It

had been the worst possible moment. Helena had been due to arrive any time, but he hadn't been able to refuse.

A prisoner had been brought into the station with facial cuts and bruises and showing signs of concussion. There was some concern as to how his injuries had occurred, but that was for the authorities to sort out. They needed him there to determine the seriousness of his condition and to advise if hospital treatment was required.

On examining the man, he decided that it was. He was confused. His pupils were dilated and his head was beginning to swell. It seemed that he had attacked someone in the street and had either got more than he'd bargained for or had received rough handling from those who'd arrested him.

Blake was impatient to get back to the practice and when the ambulance had taken the injured man to Accident and Emergency he avoided the chat that the station sergeant would have liked to have had by excusing himself with the explanation that he had someone waiting to see him.

As he drove back to the practice he was hoping that he wasn't being too presumptuous, that Helena wouldn't have been offended by his absence and would be there, waiting.

CHAPTER THREE

'HAS Helena Harris arrived?' Blake asked the receptionist on duty as he strode into the practice building.

'Yes,' he was told. 'She's in with Dr Scott.'

'And Dr Fielding?'

'Out on her rounds.'

He nodded. It was something that he and Darren should be doing, and once he'd spoken to Helena they would be off. Knowing his junior partner, he would have kept his promise to look after her to the letter. Darren was not one to pass up the chance of chatting up an attractive woman.

The door to his room was ajar and on the point of making his entrance Blake heard him say, 'So what's with you and Blake, Helena? He doesn't usually make all this fuss over a new member of staff. Are you and he seeing each other? There'll be some raised eyebrows if you are. He's been strictly on his own since he lost his wife and son. Though not for the want of offers.'

Blake's nerve ends tightened as he waited for Helena to answer. It was just like Darren to be measuring his chances the moment he met her. The cheeky young devil!

She laughed and Blake became even more tense.

'No, nothing of the kind,' she told him. 'We're neighbours, that's all. And that won't be for long as I'm moving into Blake's rented house later today. I lost my father earlier in the week and he's been very kind to me.'

'I see,' Blake heard Darren say, and he could tell from his voice that he was smiling. 'Maybe we can get together some time.'

He didn't wait to hear her answer. He'd heard enough.

'Thanks for entertaining Helena,' he said smoothly as his glance took in coffee-cups and a plate of biscuits. 'Feel free to make a start on your house calls. I won't be far behind you.'

When Darren had gone, looking somewhat sheepish, Blake said, 'My partners are both rather overpowering in their approach, but they're good doctors.'

He was furious with Darren. His junior partner hadn't known Helena five minutes and he'd come on to her. Yet he had to admit Darren was like that with all the women. A born flirt.

'I agree about the approach,' she told him wryly. 'I've had the cold shoulder from Dr Fielding and the overly warm treatment from Dr Scott. It's nice to be with someone who's normal.'

He let that pass. He wasn't feeling the least bit normal at the moment. If it wasn't so ridiculous he would say he was jealous. Of what or who he wasn't sure. She'd told Darren exactly what he'd expected her to. That he was just a good neighbour. So why was he not happy about it?

Helena was waiting for him to speak and, gathering his wits, he asked, 'So what do you think of the practice? Any change of mind?'

He wouldn't have been surprised if there had been after the way those two had behaved, but she was smiling.

'No. None. I'm looking forward to working here. Jane Benyon in particular was most welcoming. I'm sure I shall benefit from her experience. She told me that you're very selective about who you rent the cottage to, so I feel honoured.'

He was smiling, his good humour almost restored. There was just Darren's description of him still rankling. He'd made it sound as if he lived like a monk. But maybe he did.

'No need to feel like that,' he told her. 'As long as you're happy and comfortable, that's all that matters.'

She was getting to her feet and he thought that she looked better today. There was colour in her cheeks and her eyes were brighter, but who was to say that the practice Romeo wasn't responsible for that?

'I know you have lots to do, Blake,' she was saying, 'so I'll be on my way. Will I see you again before the funeral?'

She was praying he would say yes. The days stretched ahead in bleak emptiness. At the present time he was the only bright thing in her life.

Helena wasn't aware how beseeching she sounded and that he was as anxious for her company as she was for his, but he wasn't going to tell her that. In the short time that he'd known her his role had been that of protector and that was how it had to stay.

'Of course,' he told her. 'You can see me whenever you want. You know where I live and if I'm not at the house I'm here. I don't get much further than that. And isn't there something you've forgotten that we're both involved in?'

'What?'

'You're supposed to be moving into that house of mine today, aren't you? If you can hang on until this evening, I'll give you some assistance.'

Helena smiled. She'd been hoping he would offer but had had no intention of asking.

'It will be mostly clothes and toiletries that I'm taking…and Dad's papers.'

'Fine, then it won't take us long,' he said.

From the moment she stepped into the cottage Helena felt better. The safe house had possessed a glut of locks and alarms but it had been short on home comforts and in the cosy confines of her new home she was happy to put its utilitarian decor behind her.

As she explored the rooms with a smile on her face Blake was watching her.

'So will it do?' he asked.

'Yes.' She beamed. 'It's heaven to get away from that place. I might have a housewarming. Would you come if I did? It would be just the two of us as I don't know anyone else.'

He was laughing.

'Yes, of course I'll come. But you *do* know some other people now that you've been introduced at the surgery. Darren and Maxine, for instance.' She pulled a face. 'And Jane and Beverley.'

'I suppose so,' she agreed, 'but I don't know them like I know you.'

She watched his eyes darken and his mouth curve softly and wondered what construction he was putting on that comment, but he wasn't to be drawn.

'I'm afraid I have to go, Helena,' he said. 'I have an engagement. Maxine's son is having a twenty-first party. She's divorced and his father won't be there, so I've been invited as a sort of stand-in.'

'Oh! I'm sorry if I've delayed you,' she said.

'Don't be. I'm in plenty of time. Sleep tight in your new home. I'll see you soon.' And off he went.

When he'd gone she had a quick bite and then went to sit in the cottage's small back garden. It was a warm evening and the sun was setting like a golden ball of fire on the horizon. What was Blake's relationship with his strident partner? she wondered yet again. Maybe he saw qualities in her that were not visible to herself. She would have to look long and deep to find any likable traits in Maxine Fielding.

When the sun had gone and dusk lay over the garden she got to her feet. If she was going to live here it was time she got to know the area, she decided. Locking the door securely behind her, she made her way to the Swan Hotel just down the road.

The first person she saw in the bar was Darren Scott and she wished she'd stayed at home. He saw her and came across. She dredged up a smile.

'Hello, there,' he said. 'Nice to see you again. Can I buy you a drink?'

'Er…no, thanks,' she said hurriedly, feeling instinctively that it would be a mistake to take him up on the offer. 'I just came in to check what sort of food they serve here in case I want to eat out any time, but tonight I'm intending to have an early night.'

At that moment a group of his friends came in and she made her escape, deciding as she did so that the Swan wasn't going to be a regular place of call for her if Darren hung out there. He seemed likable enough, but he wasn't Blake.

Instead of going straight back to the house, Helena found a supermarket open for late-night purchases and dawdling along the aisles she did a leisurely shop.

When she got back to the house she went from room to room, drawing the curtains, and as she was pulling them across in the dining room she saw that a white van that she'd seen earlier was still parked in a lane overlooking the back garden.

She'd thought nothing of it when she'd seen it before. There'd been a man sitting behind the wheel, smoking, and she'd thought he must be waiting for someone in one of the other cottages. But now, an hour and a half later, she saw from the light of the streetlamp that he was still there.

Her new found feeling of security was oozing away like water down a grid. He was watching the house, she thought. Had someone followed her there? Been lurking at the other place and watched her move in here?

It couldn't be so, she told herself firmly. Blake had assured her that the witness protection scheme left no margin for error. She was letting her imagination run riot.

Once in bed she couldn't sleep. She was drawn to the window and every time she looked out the van was still there, headlights dimmed and the dark shadow of the driver filling the night with menace.

There was a flash from a camera and she thought fearfully that he was taking pictures, but why, for heaven's sake? Was it for the benefit of someone else? So that *they* would know where to find her?

Suddenly she couldn't stand it any longer. Terror had her in its grip. She had to ring Blake. It was one o'clock. Would he be back from the party?

Blake had passed the cottage on his way home from Maxine's, seen that all the lights were out and had driven past. If there'd been any signs of life he would have called in. Five minutes with Helena would have taken away the taste that an evening spent with Maxine had left. But the last thing his new lodger needed was someone banging on her door at past midnight. She was happy in her new home, felt safe there, and he didn't want to do anything to spoil that.

Those sentiments lasted until the phone rang as he was climbing the stairs to bed. He groaned. Not a patient! The emergency service was supposed to deal with night calls.

When he picked up the receiver Helena's voice spoke in his ear.

'Blake! There's someone watching the house,' she croaked. 'In a white van at the back. He's got a camera...been there for hours.'

'What?' he exclaimed. 'Is everywhere locked up?'

'Yes, but that won't stop him, will it?'

'I'm on my way, Helena,' he said. 'I'll ring the police and then I'll be with you in minutes.'

He couldn't believe it. He'd been at such pains to convince her she was safe and he'd been wrong. If anything happened to her he would never forgive himself. Some protector he'd turned out to be!

The van was there, just as Helena had said, and there was a fellow dozing behind the wheel. Flinging himself out of his car, Blake wrenched open the door of the vehicle and dragged him out.

'Hey! What's going on?' the nocturnal watcher bellowed.

'You tell me,' Blake growled. 'You're watching my friend's house, aren't you?'

'Depends who your friend is. If it's the lady at the end house, yes, I am. I'm a private detective. Her husband works nights and he's hired me to watch what she gets up to when he's not there.'

As Blake's hold on the front of his shirt slackened, the man said, 'You thought I was up to no good, did you? Sorry to disappoint you. Just doing my job. I have a licence.'

At that moment the police arrived and after explanations all round and no mention on Blake's part of the witness protection programme, he went to see Helena.

When she opened the door to him he held out his arms and she went into them like a homing bird.

'I was wrong, wasn't I?' she groaned against his chest. 'I've been watching through the window and saw that it was all a mistake. What was he doing there?'

Blake was stroking her hair.

'The fellow was a private detective, keeping an eye on an erring wife in one of the other houses.'

'Oh, no! And I dragged you out of bed for that. You must think me completely neurotic.'

He placed a finger under her chin and lifted her face to his.

'I wasn't in bed and, no, I don't think you're neurotic. I think you're brave and beautiful.'

'I wish I were,' she told him regretfully. 'You must rue the day you took me under your wing. I promise to keep my outsize imagination in check in future.'

He was laughing.

'One thing is for sure. The lady who was under surveillance will have latched onto what was going on after all that rumpus in the back lane. I can't see the private eye getting paid after that.'

She was laughing herself now.

'Fancy having a *white* van. He's not going to be inconspicuous in that, is he?'

'No. I'm afraid not.'

Blake would have liked to have lingered. He'd wanted to see her and the opportunity had presented itself, but it would be taking advantage of her vulnerability again if he did so, putting her gently from him, he said, 'Will you be able to sleep now?'

Her smile was rueful.

'Yes. You were right and I was wrong. In future I'll have to have more confidence in what you tell me.'

'I don't blame you for having your doubts,' he told her, 'but enough for one night. Go back to bed, Helena, and I'll see you soon.'

She nodded obediently and as the door shut behind him Blake thought wryly that they were becoming close for all the wrong reasons. He wanted Helena to be drawn to him for himself, not as the man who kept putting things right for her.

Climbing the stairs again, Helena was thinking similar thoughts. She didn't want to be amongst those Blake felt responsible for. She wanted him to see her as a desirable woman rather than a nervous encumbrance.

As she snuggled beneath the bed covers once more she vowed that tonight was the last time she called upon him for help. It was time she got a grip on herself and returned to normality, became the sane uncomplicated person who had returned from Australia, with the only problem in her life the news that her father had moved house.

In the days before the funeral Blake had little time to spare. It was all systems go as usual at the practice and even more so because Maxine had taken a few days' leave to coincide with her son's twenty-first.

He sensed that Jane Benyon was feeling under pressure, too, as the other practice nurse, who was leaving shortly, was too lovestruck to be of much use, which meant that he wasn't the only one looking forward to Helena's arrival.

The police had called him out one lunchtime to a prisoner who'd been having a severe asthma attack in the cells behind the Crown Court and that had taken a slice out of his day.

It had been a woman who'd received a heavy sentence for embezzling a large sum of money from her employers and when they'd taken her down to the cells the asthma attack had started.

She'd been blue in the face, wheezing heavily and sweating with the effort to breathe. Her heartbeat had been rapid and Blake had been aware that in an attack of this severity the recommended dosage of a bronchodilator drug would not have been enough to bring relief. He'd repeated the dose and still the woman had been gasping, which had left him with no alternative but to have her admitted to hospital.

Yet in the midst of all the matters that had claimed him he hadn't forgotten Helena and he'd phoned her each day to make sure that all was well.

'Yes,' she assured him each time. 'I'm sorting out Dad's affairs and generally settling down into my new surroundings. How is everything with you?'

'Fine,' he told her, happy to hear the sound of her voice. 'Except that there aren't enough hours in the day at the moment. Maxine is taking some leave and the police called me out. All I need now is for the Prison Service to request my presence.'

'The Prison Service?' she echoed hollowly. 'I'm not with you.'

'I'm contracted to them for inmates who are taken ill on the premises, or have been hospitalised and once back behind bars need post-operative care. The prison has its own clinic with a resident doctor, but GPs like myself are called in from the outside to treat sick inmates.'

'You never told me you were involved in that,' she said.

'Well, exactly. I would have thought you'd heard enough about crime and criminals since you came home, without details of prison through the eyes of a suburban GP.'

'So, is working for the Prison Service part of the police surgeon's routine?'

'No. They're separate contracts, but quite a few GPs are involved with both because the function is similar and if one does feel this kind of commitment then the satisfaction is twofold.

'But getting back to basics. Regarding the funeral, I'll call round on Sunday night for a quick chat about the arrangements if that's all right with you.'

'Yes, of course,' she told him, her voice lifting.

She was dreading what lay ahead and every moment spent with Blake helped her to face up to the grim reality of it. How she would have felt without his support was something she couldn't contemplate.

The sun was still in the sky when he arrived on Sunday evening, and when Helena opened the door to him he said, 'Do you feel like a walk?'

She smiled.

'Yes. I do. I've been cooped up inside for too long.'

'Me, too,' he agreed, and as she locked the door behind them he said, 'No more scares, I hope.'

'No,' she told him, eyes dancing. 'I don't run a mile when the milkman calls or the postman, and I even stood my ground when a double-glazing salesman tried to sell me his wares.'

'Great stuff,' he said laughingly. 'Your dad would be proud of you. I know I am.' He sobered suddenly. 'After tomorrow you'll feel better, too. The period between a death and the funeral is like being in a sad and bewildered state of limbo. Almost all of us feel better when we've laid to rest those we love.'

'Was that how you felt?'

He didn't say either yes or no.

'In my case it was two funerals,' was his only comment, and there wasn't much she could say to follow that.

As if to shrug off the sombre moment, he said, 'So are you all set for Tuesday? It will seem strange to see you in uniform.'

'I can't wait,' she told him with a fervour that he thought showed the degree of her loneliness. He wasn't going to speculate on any other reason for it. For the present Helena's safety and peace of mind had to come first and any other crazy imaginings he might have put on hold.

As they walked along in the summer evening it was clear that they weren't the only ones who'd been tempted out. They could hear the thud of balls on nearby tennis courts, the beer garden at the back of the Swan was full and there was plenty of traffic on the roads.

Suddenly the screech of a motorbike's brakes came from behind them and as they turned at the sound the bike collided with a car that had come out of a side road.

'Oh, no!' Blake cried. 'Come on, Helena. It looks like big trouble for the guy on the bike.'

They were the first on the scene and saw immediately that the slim helmeted figure had come off worst. He was lying very still and as Blake undid his leather jacket with urgent fingers Helena saw that his chest was oozing blood.

'He's breathing,' she said, 'but only just, and from the angle of his limbs I think we have some fractures.'

Blake nodded. 'Phone for an ambulance while I check that his tongue isn't blocking his airway.'

While she was making the call Helena ran across to where the elderly car driver was slumped behind the wheel, gazing straight ahead in deep shock but apparently uninjured.

It seemed as if he'd come out of the side road without checking that the way had been clear. The bike had had the right of way, which made her think that in these sorts of incidents prudence didn't always walk hand in hand with age.

'They're on their way,' she said, dropping to her knees beside Blake.

He didn't reply. His eyes were on the biker's chest. There was no rise and fall.

'We're losing him, Helena,' he muttered. 'We're going to have to resuscitate. Ready! You do the cardiac compressions and I'll do the mouth-to-mouth.'

As she did five compressions to Blake's every breath there was a feeling of amazing oneness. They were a team. If they could save the motorcyclist's life what a reward it would be for all their years of training, and if they couldn't...

She wasn't going to think about that. Her eyes were watching for any movement of the man's chest. At last it came and as their glances locked in relieved triumph she heard the siren of an approaching ambulance.

'We had cardiac arrest but he's back with us,' Blake told the paramedics as they leapt from the ambulance. 'There are serious chest injuries, if the blood loss is anything to go by, and possible fractures of the arms.'

The motorist was still sitting in the driver's seat but while they'd been treating the motorcyclist a crowd had gathered and some of them were hovering anxiously around him.

'He's in deep shock,' Helena told the ambulance crew. 'We weren't able to get to him as the biker was so desperately in need of help.'

'What *are* you two?' one of the paramedics asked as they carefully stretchered the injured youth into the ambulance.

'A doctor and nurse out for a quiet stroll,' Blake told him with a wry smile.

'Right. Well, it was certainly this guy's lucky day,' the paramedic observed.

'Yes, it was,' Helena agreed. 'Just make sure you keep him breathing.'

As the vehicle clanged off into the night a second ambulance came for the car driver, and as he was slowly helped out from behind the crushed bonnet a paramedic said, 'We're taking him in for observation. He's looking a bit blue round the mouth.'

When they had gone the crowd dispersed and Helena and Blake were left to make their way home.

'It's a marvellous feeling, being in the right place at the right time, isn't it?' she said.

'Yes, it is,' he agreed, and thought that this wasn't the only time he'd been fortunate to be in the right place. He'd been there for her and would continue to be so if she would let him.

When they got back to the cottage Helena said, 'Do you want to come in and wash? We're both a bit gory.'

'Yes, why not?' he answered easily. 'We still haven't talked about tomorrow, have we?'

'No,' she said soberly. 'Death and disaster seem to be everywhere, don't they? I hope when we make enquiries about the biker there is some good news.'

'It won't be that good,' Blake pointed out. 'His injuries were serious.'

'Yes, but as long as he's alive, that it doesn't end up that he went for a ride and never came back.'

The funeral was over. In a plain black dress, relieved only by a fine gold chain, and with a broad-brimmed black hat to match, Helena had shed no tears during the simple yet sombre service at a church not far from the practice. But she'd gripped Blake's hand as if she would never let it go as the words had been said and she'd still held onto him tightly as they'd stood at the graveside afterwards.

And now they were back at the cottage, having a quick bite before Blake returned to the practice for the late afternoon surgery. She seemed more tranquil now, he thought. As if with the laying to rest of her father she had said goodbye to one part of her life and was now ready to face the future.

Blake knew there would still be dark days ahead. He'd been there himself. The distress from the suddenness of James Harris's death and the circumstances under which she'd found him living wouldn't disappear overnight, but she could look forward now and if it all worked out to plan he would be there for her during the first difficult months.

He wasn't sure what would happen after that and thought wryly that at the present time Helena probably saw the future more clearly than he did as she would have no idea how she was affecting him.

'Let me take you for a drink tonight to toast the new job,' he suggested as he was about to leave.

She shook her head.

It would be so easy to say yes, it was what she wanted to say, but Blake had done enough. He couldn't be expected to support her any longer. He had his own life to lead and, if his comments about her wanting to move on once she was feeling better were anything to go by, he wasn't expecting her to be featuring in his affairs for any length of time.

He was eyeing her questioningly. 'No?'

She managed a smile but it was a weak affair and so was the excuse that followed it.

'I think I should have an early night so that I'll be poised for action in the morning.'

It wasn't what she really thought. Some prime time with Blake would be fantastic after the week's sombre happenings. But common sense was telling her that she could be heading for more hurt if she started reading more into his concern for her than she should.

'All right,' he said easily. 'An early night it is. And now I really must get back to the practice or Maxine will be throwing a wobbly.' He touched her cheek for a fleeting moment. 'The worst of the nightmare is over now, Helena. Of course the grief remains, but it really will get less with time. I know. I've been there. And though no one can ever replace those we've lost, life does go on.'

'Will you ever marry again?' she asked impulsively, and was immediately horrified at having asked such a question.

To her relief he was smiling.

'Maybe. If the right person came along. They haven't so far.'

'So it's not Dr Fielding?'

He was frowning now and she knew she'd gone too far.

'It's not anyone at the moment,' he told her coolly, while thinking that it soon could be if the spell she was weaving around him became any more binding. But he could imagine Helena's reaction if he told her how he felt with her father barely cold in his grave. She would think he was an opportunist!

In the early evening Helena was restless and knew why. She was wishing she'd accepted Blake's invitation and put pride to one side. But the deed was done and the hours stretched emptily ahead.

At nine o'clock she could stand the inactivity no longer and, changing out of her mourning clothes, she put on a lightweight jacket and trousers and set off in the direction of the Swan.

It might seem irreverent to be dressed up like this and in the pub on the night of the funeral, she thought, but her dad would have understood. He would know that she was desperate to get back to normality because her life had been far from 'normal' during past days. She was part of a law-abiding family and to be innocently involved with the wrongdoings of others was the last thing she wanted.

Blake was used to dealing with criminals. Maybe he thought her horror was a bit overdone, but she'd never seen the inside of a police cell or a prison, even as a visitor, and never wanted to.

Darren and his friends were crowded around the pool table when she walked in and remembering how aloof she'd been the last time they'd met in there she smiled and it had him immediately making a beeline for her.

Within seconds he'd drawn her into the crowd that he was with. They were a friendly, noisy lot and Helena began to relax. She was laughing at something one of them had said when she looked up and saw Blake coming through the door.

Her face went scarlet. She should have anticipated that he might appear, she told herself, though for some reason she hadn't expected him to have been referring to this place when he'd suggested taking her for a drink.

What she'd thought didn't matter now. He was here and observing her unsmilingly from across the room. Bracing herself, she went slowly across to where he was standing.

'I changed my mind,' she said awkwardly. 'There suddenly seemed to be a lot of hours to get through before morning.'

He sighed and it made her feel as if she was being tiresome.

'You don't have to explain your movements to me,' he said, as if she were a wayward child. 'It's only natural for you to want to be with people of your own age.'

Helena stared at him. What was he on about? The people she was with were just folk to chat to, casual company, including Darren, and if he had any ideas to the contrary she would soon put him right.

Blake was making himself sound like Methuselah and once again she sensed the inference that he saw the support he'd given her as more of a duty than a pleasure.

'Your friends are waiting for you,' he said in the same tone of mild admonition. 'Don't let me detain you.' Leaving her with no reply to that, he went into the restaurant.

She was next on the pool table and found she could no more hit the ball with the cue than fly to the moon. Darren hadn't helped by asking what she and Blake had been discussing, and after that she'd been all fingers and thumbs.

As soon as the game was over she made a quick departure. Once back at the cottage, Helena had to face up to the fact that Blake's opinion of her mattered. Mattered a lot, and after the way he'd helped her through the ordeal of the funeral he must have thought her ungrateful to turn up at the pub after she'd refused his invitation.

Alternatively, he might have been relieved. Maybe she was setting too much store on herself in thinking he'd been disappointed. She was going to have to control her feelings, she decided as she climbed the stairs to bed.

Tomorrow was 'D' day, the beginning of the rest of her life, and she was glad. Glad that Blake was going to be part of it in whatever role he chose to be. And if he was expecting her stay at the Priory Practice to be brief, he was in for a surprise. If he wanted to get rid of her he would have to throw her out.

So that was that, Blake thought as he waited to be served. If he'd wanted signs that he'd served his purpose and proof that Helena was more comfortable in the company of people of her own age, he'd got it. And he'd let her see that he had.

Yet there were only eight years between them. It was the hand that life had dealt him that made him feel older. It was understandable that a workaholic widower like himself wasn't going to be the ideal companion for a woman like her. He'd only seen her at her most subdued, but he sensed that there were depths to her that he had yet to see and it wasn't going to be easy, standing by and doing nothing. He was a man of action in every way except in his private life, and it sometimes felt as if that had been frozen in time.

CHAPTER FOUR

HELENA awoke the next morning to the realisation that the previous night's happenings had taken the edge off her anticipation regarding the job. The last thing she wanted was to be at odds with Blake.

He'd seemed reasonable enough when they'd spoken but she felt that the incident had shown her up in a bad light, that she'd given the impression she didn't want his company when the truth of it was that she couldn't see enough of him.

Well, that would be rectified today, she thought. From now on they would be seeing a great deal of each other in the busy confines of the practice, but where she'd been eagerly looking forward to it before now she wasn't sure.

'You won't get any special concessions from me if you take the job,' he'd told her when it had first been mentioned, and she'd been quick to assure him that she wouldn't want any. Those sentiments hadn't changed, but neither did she want to feel that she was being tolerated, because from the moment she'd opened the door to him on that dreadful morning he'd been lumbered with her.

Play it by ear, she told herself as she showered and dressed. If Blake is cool with you after last night, keep your distance, be polite but not pushy, and if he's his usual friendly self...be grateful.

As Blake drove to the practice he was facing up to the fact that he'd been jealous the night before...again. When he'd seen Helena laughing up at one of the young men in the pub he'd felt as if something had hit him hard in the chest.

Yet he'd had to do the noble thing, hadn't he? Make out that he had one foot in the grave compared to Helena and the group she was with, when all the time he'd wanted to carry her off somewhere so that he could have her to himself.

It didn't make for a good working relationship if he was going to be like this every time
she smiled at another man. So why not do
something about it? the voice of reason asked.
But what?

Sweep her off her feet? Hardly, in the present climate. All he'd done for her had been
because of genuine concern and any change of
attitude might make her think he'd had a hid-
den agenda. Businesslike and brisk would have
to be the order of the day for the time being
with no inkling of his real feelings.

She was there before him, parking the car
that had been her father's on the forecourt of
the practice.

'Good morning, Nurse,' he said, keeping to
his new resolve and immediately wishing he
hadn't when he saw her chastened expression.
But she was rallying.

'Good morning...Dr Pemberton,' she said
coolly, feeling as if they were playing some
sort of silly game. 'Shall I report to you or
Jane?'

'I suggest that you go straight to the nurses'
room,' he suggested in the same tone. 'You're

already acquainted with everyone so there's no need for introductions.'

So this is how it's going to be, she thought. Was she being given the impersonal treatment because of protocol or because of last night? If it was for the first reason, fine, but if it was a backlash from the night before, her first day was going to go down like a damp squib.

Surprisingly it didn't. From the moment she presented herself and was met by the woman who would be sharing the duties of practice nurse with her, Helena felt at home.

If Blake was going to be all official she wasn't going to let it get her down, she decided. He was senior partner and entitled to keep her at a distance if he wanted to. As long as he was willing to put up with her she would accept what looked like being the end of one relationship and the beginning of another. That was satisfactory in its own way, but not likely to make her blood warm.

As the morning progressed Jane explained the surgery routine to her and gave her a running commentary on the rest of the staff. For Blake she had nothing but praise.

'Dr Pemberton drives himself too hard,' she told Helena. 'It's as if he doesn't want time to think. But it's three years since he lost his wife and child. We all wish he could meet someone and be happy again.'

There was no comment forthcoming from her listener. Helena was remembering how she'd asked him about that very thing and he hadn't had a lot to say.

The verdict on Maxine was that she wasn't popular with the staff. She was too bossy and Darren, although a nice man, was too fresh.

'We see the expectant mums on Tuesday afternoons,' Jane told her, 'diabetes patients on Wednesdays and the asthma clinic is on Fridays. We practice nurses take turns to assist whichever of the partners is in charge.

'Dr Pemberton told me that you've just lost your father and live alone as you have no family nearby,' her new colleague commented when they stopped for a quick coffee in the middle of the morning. 'My house isn't far from his rented cottage and any time you feel like some company you'll be most welcome.

It's no joke moving house when you don't know anyone, is it?'

Helena could have told her that she'd lived in *two* strange houses in the space of a fortnight. That the first of them had belonged to the witness protection scheme and that the second, in a different kind of way, was also a place of protection.

The man who had offered it to her was in a room across the passage, attending to his patients. Fulfilling the pledges he'd made to the sick who were free to consult him, and ever ready to go to those who had forfeited their freedom for one reason or another and needed his skills.

But there was no way she would ever tell anyone about her recent nightmare. He was the only one who knew and she would trust him with her life. Out of the horrific mess that she'd come home to there was only one good thing...Blake Pemberton.

As Blake had watched Helena settling in as if she'd worked in the practice for ever, his earlier sombre mood diminished. She wasn't going to let him down, he thought. There would be no cause for the other partners to question his judgement. As he called in his first patient of the day, he thanked the fates that had provided a vacancy for a nurse at just the right moment.

One of his patients, an elderly, infirm lady, was showing signs of anaemia and he took her across to the nurses' room for blood tests himself, instead of sending her to wait outside until one of them was available to attend to her.

'So how's it going?' he asked in a low voice as Jane saw to the patient.

His glance was taking in Helena's trim slenderness in the neat blue uniform, the healthier colour in her cheeks and the candid gaze from the beautiful green eyes which had been the first thing to register when they'd been thrown into each other's lives.

'Fine,' she replied levelly, not sure if protocol was still the order of the day, then added, with her voice warming, 'Jane is making me very welcome.' As if she'd tuned in to his earlier thinking, she went on, 'I won't let you down, Blake...ever.'

The firm line of his mouth softened and though his answering smile was hardly a beam it reached the dark eyes looking into hers. In that moment, on the heels of the promise she'd just made him, Helena knew that she loved this man and would for all time. But until she could be sure he wouldn't think she was letting gratitude sweep her along into something she was mistaking for passion, she would bask in the wonder of it alone and hope that soon he would begin to see her as something other than one of his good causes.

'I must go,' he said. 'There are still a few patients waiting to be seen. You know where I am if you have any problems.'

She nodded. The words had a lovely feeling to them. 'You know where I am.' May that always be the case, she prayed.

The practice must have been sending out letters about tetanus boosters for those who'd last had the jab ten years ago or longer, and the next patient waiting for the nurses had come in response to the reminder.

Jane left Helena to deal with it while she went downstairs to find some old records relating to a patient who was questioning treatment she'd received some years ago. It wasn't on the current files and by the time she came back it was lunchtime.

'So you've arrived, I see.' Maxine said when she came into the nurses' room in the early afternoon. She'd been out during the morning but, it seemed, was now about to make her presence felt.

Helena didn't reply. It had been a statement rather than a question.

'I believe you're renting Blake's house.'

Again the same kind of comment but, having no wish to antagonise the abrasive woman on her first day, Helena replied. 'Yes. I am.' And thought that Maxine would surely prefer that to her being his next-door neighbour.

She wondered what the other woman would think if she knew the true circumstances of why Blake had offered her the house. If Maxine was aware that she had inadvertently been caught up on the edge of the criminal fraternity, innocent or not, she didn't think she would come out of it looking too good as far as the other woman was concerned.

But the female partner of the practice wasn't going to find out about that. No one was. Now that the shock of it was beginning to lessen, there was anger inside her at the thought of her father's integrity having put him at risk as it had.

All right, he'd died from natural causes, but who was to say that the stress of the court case and what followed it hadn't contributed to the cardiac arrest? Yet Helena knew if ever *she* found herself in the same position of having to testify in court for the sake of justice, she would do it. She owed it to her parents and her upbringing.

She believed that Blake would agree with her reasoning. He was a man of integrity like her father had been. But she was debating a situation that was hardly likely to arise, so did it really matter what his thoughts would be on it?

Bringing her mind back to the present, she found Maxine's calculating gaze still upon her, but to Helena's relief the brief inquisition

seemed to be over as the other woman explained the real reason for her presence in the
nurses' room.

'One of my patients is waiting to be seen by
you,' she said. 'I want an ESR blood test done.
There are acute muscular problems. She has
recently been bereaved and is in a very dis-
tressed condition so treat her gently.' To
Helena's amazement she added, 'Being in the
same position yourself, I'm sure you can understand.'

When Maxine had gone back to her own
room Jane said, 'That's Dr Fielding. Strange
as it may seem, a heart *does* beat somewhere
beneath all the prickles.' She grinned. 'And I
have a feeling that its beat is always faster
when Dr Pemberton is around.'

Helena nodded. It was a conclusion she'd
already come to. But Blake was far too special
to be hooked up to that woman. Yet he had
stood in for his father at her son's twenty-first
and Maxine had called round as if she were a
regular visitor that night when she herself had
been sleeping in his spare room.

Don't think about it, she told herself. The day is going well, don't spoil it. It was good to have her mind occupied. She'd done too much brooding lately, more than she'd ever done in her life. To be back in health care was wonderful, and what made it even more so was that all the time she was at the surgery Blake wasn't far away.

Helena was tired that evening but it was from a day well spent, and as she took her meal out to the small terrace at the back of the cottage she eyed the now deserted lane at the bottom of the garden whimsically.

She'd really panicked that night but thankfully it had turned out to be a domestic dispute. If it hadn't been, Blake would have made short work of the watcher so concerned had he been on her behalf.

What was he doing now? she wondered. Eating his solitary evening meal like she was? She'd seen little of him during the afternoon. He'd been out on house visits and then there'd been the late surgery.

He'd been deep in discussion with Maxine and Darren when she and Jane had left, and he'd saluted them briefly without comment.

But she was quite sure that he would either call or ring later in the evening to ask how her first day had gone. She was gradually feeling more normal, not as much in limbo, and it was all due to him.

Was loving him going to be everything she wanted it to be? she pondered dreamily as bees buzzed amongst the flowers and a blackbird hopped around at her feet. Or would it be a fraught and rocky road with lots of twists and turnings? It would be if he didn't feel the same, and so far he had given no sign that he found her anything other than a stranger who'd walked into a nightmare.

She'd been in his arms a few times. There'd been that first morning when he'd come to break the news of her father's death, and that same night when he'd held her as she'd cried out in her sleep. And again he'd held her close on the night when he'd come rushing round because of the white van.

But each time he'd been offering comfort and reassurance rather than passion. Just as when she'd clung to him at the funeral and on the occasion when he'd gently touched her cheek.

Today everything had changed. She wanted to feel his kisses, his arms around her, knowing it was where she belonged, and it was incredible. Only a short time ago she hadn't even known Blake existed and now…now he was all she could think of and it had nothing to do with gratitude.

Helena wished that her father could have known Blake, but sadly it had been because of his death that she had got to know the man who'd captured her heart. Yet she felt that somewhere her father would be smiling his approval, while at the same time reminding her that as yet the romance was a one-sided affair.

That was brought home to her even more as the evening wore on and there was no word from Blake. For all she knew, he might be with Maxine or some other person that she hadn't even heard of, Helena told herself. Or just relaxing after a busy day in the knowledge that she was now sorted. Employed, housed and looking forward instead of back.

She wasn't to know it but Blake was having his own share of frustration as the evening wore on. He'd been the last one to leave the practice and was just about to lock up when he had a phone call to say that he was required at the police station. A break-in had gone wrong at a big house in the area and the culprit had been apprehended with great enthusiasm by the owner, a well-known rugby player.

Having bitten off more than he could chew, the wrongdoer was protesting about cuts and bruises and a possible fracture of the collar bone, and the police were asking that Blake treat him in the cells and advise on how serious his injuries were with a view to a charge of assault being brought against the outraged house-owner.

He'd seen that kind of thing before, he thought sombrely as he drove the short distance to the station, the victim ending up on the wrong side of the law because they'd tried to protect themselves and their property. But if the thief was injured his wellbeing had to be seen to.

The cuts and bruises turned out to be superficial but the collar bone was almost certainly broken and a visit to Accident and Emergency under police escort was called for.

Driving by the side of the park on his way back, Blake saw Emily Sutton, a sprightly pensioner who was one of his patients. She was bobbing along by the flower-beds when she suddenly tripped and fell onto the concrete pathway.

Stopping the car, he pushed his way through the bushes and went to help her. She was lying with her arm bent beneath her and her face was ashen as she looked up at him.

'Dr Pemberton,' she quavered. 'Where have you come from?'

'I was driving past and saw you fall, Emily,' he told her. 'Where are you hurt?'

'It's my wrist. I fell with all my weight on it.'

He helped her carefully to her feet, brushed dead leaves off her coat, then gently examined her wrist.

'I think we'd better get you to Accident and Emergency to have it X-rayed. I'll take you there, I'm going that way.'

While Emily was being examined a little later, Blake phoned Helena.

'I was on my way to your place,' he told her, 'but I saw one of my elderly patients fall in the park and I've brought her to A and E to have her wrist X-rayed. So in case you thought I wasn't keen to hear how your first day went, that's the reason.'

Her face had brightened at the sound of his voice.

'I see. Have you eaten?'

'Er, no. I'll get around to it eventually. I was on my way back from the police station.'

'How long are you going to be there, Blake?'

'At least an hour, I would think. If the wrist is broken, and I'm pretty sure it is, Emily will have to have a cast on it, which all takes time, and then I'll have to take her home and see her settled.'

'That's really nice of you. You could have just sent for an ambulance.'

'Yes, I know, but that might have meant her being here for hours. It would have done her more harm than good.'

Twenty minutes later Helena appeared by his side.

'I've brought you some food,' she said. 'Prepared with my own fair hands.'

'Sounds interesting.'

'Not really. Just a salad sandwich and a doughnut. Where's Emily?'

'Getting plastered and I don't mean that the poor old dear is in the bar.'

'I should hope not,' Helena exclaimed in mock horror.

He smiled.

'Now that she's got over the shock she's quite enjoying all the fuss. A young nurse is looking after her and Social Services will be getting involved. If they think she will be at risk on her own tonight, they might keep her in.'

At that moment they appeared, and as if she'd read his mind the nurse said, 'We're going to keep Mrs Sutton in overnight, Dr Pemberton, and then tomorrow a social worker will come to see her, just to make sure she can cope.'

'We're going to go now, Emily,' he told her. 'If you have any problems with the wrist when you get home, send for me.'

'You didn't have to come chasing round here,' Blake told Helena when they got outside, 'but I'm glad you did. I'm not used to having anyone take an interest in my welfare. It's quite a pleasant feeling.'

'So doesn't Maxine have your wellbeing at heart?'

'Er…no,' he responded drily. 'But I don't want to talk about her. I'm interested to know how your first day at the practice went.'

'Fine,' she told him breezily. 'I'm going to love it there.'

There was a moment's silence and she wondered if Blake was taken aback by her enthusiasm. After all he'd twice made it plain that he wasn't expecting her to stay.

'Good,' he said at last. 'Especially as I talked you into it.'

'If you recall, I didn't need any persuading,' she told him with a catch in her voice. 'I owe you a lot, Blake.'

'Nonsense,' he said firmly. 'Just keep up the good work and I'll be happy.'

So that was all he required of her, she thought glumly. That she could do the job. She felt like a deflated balloon, but under the circumstances was he likely to say anything more exciting? He would have no idea that she was in love with him.

As they made their way to their cars Blake was smiling. So his green-eyed protégée liked the job. It was a step in the right direction. Maybe in time, when Helena had got over the shock of her father's death, she might see him as someone more important than a good Samaritan.

He wasn't to know that it had already happened and in the days that followed he treated her with a brisk friendliness that made her think that the chances of him ever returning her feelings were remote.

Darren Scott was another matter. He was an outrageous flirt in a lighthearted sort of way and as long as he kept it like that she didn't mind.

Then one day he came breezing in while she was changing the disposable sheets on the examination couch in his room and commented that the latest batch to be delivered ripped easily and were of substandard quality.

'Try them and you'll see what I mean,' he said, and so she got onto the couch and wriggled around, digging in heels and elbows to see if it would tear. He came across and, bending over her so that their faces were almost touching and gazing into her eyes, said, 'So what do you think?'

She 'thought' that he was just a bit too near for comfort and was about to remove herself from such close proximity when Blake came in.

'With regard to what we were saying earlier about Mrs Thompson's treatment...' he was saying with his glance on the paperwork in his hand, then he looked up. 'What on earth is going on here?' he bellowed.

'We were testing the sheets,' Helena told him unconvincingly.

'So it would seem. Is this before, or after? I'd be obliged if you'd keep those sorts of antics for after working hours.'

Helena's face flamed as she raised herself to a sitting position. She glared at Darren, but he was grinning widely and she realised furiously that he obviously found the situation highly amusing.

As Blake strode back to where he'd come from she said stonily, 'You did that on purpose, didn't you? They're no different to any other disposable products we've had. You wanted Blake to catch us. Why?'

'Just to see if he's as taken with you as I think he is,' he said with the grin still in evidence.

'You are the limit!' she told him, thinking that she might have seen the funny side of it, too, if it hadn't involved Blake and herself. 'It's time you found yourself a good woman who will keep you in check.'

'And you're not offering?'

'No. I'm not!'

He sighed.

'Right. So I'd better go and start my calls, then.'

'Yes, do that,' she told him, and went back to the nurses' room to straighten out her ruffled feathers.

Surely Blake didn't think she would be playing those sorts of games in the surgery? she thought. And with Darren of all people. He was a flirt and previously harmless, but after today she would be watching him. Her love for Blake was the most important thing in her life. She couldn't bear that anything should tarnish it. Surely he knew her better than that. But did he? They hadn't known each other all that long. Was he thinking there were depths to her that he didn't want to plumb?

When he came in to tell her that Emily Sutton was now home, being monitored by Social Services, and would be coming in to have a cut dressed, which she'd sustained in the fall, Helena listened to what he had to say and then as he turned to go said quickly, 'That was just a joke on Darren's part, Blake. You know what he's like.'

His set expression didn't alter. 'Yes. I do. And if it was a joke, what was behind it?'

'It was for your benefit.'

'I wouldn't say there was much benefit to be had from where I was standing.'

She swallowed hard. 'He was trying to wind you up. He wanted to see if it would get to you, er…seeing us together.'

'I see. So because I didn't pat you both on the head, the verdict is that it *did* get to me. Is that it?'

'Sort of,' she said lamely, wishing Darren a million miles away. She was aghast. Where had the trust and friendship between them suddenly disappeared to? She felt tears prick. Never could she have envisaged herself bickering like this with Blake. He was her sun, moon and stars, and he was turning it all into darkness.

But the injustice of it was rankling and, unable to help herself, she flared, 'You've lived on your own for too long. It's made you narrow and judgemental.'

The tears were sparkling on her lashes. 'You should know I wouldn't ever do anything to hurt or annoy you after all that you've done for me.'

His face softened.

'You're right, Helena. I *am* out of touch. Meeting you has made me realise it.'

He took a step towards her and when she saw the purpose in his eyes her heartbeat quickened. As his arms came around her, his mouth was upon hers. She kissed him back and he almost swung her off her feet, and the sun, moon and stars appeared again as she gave herself up to the exquisite pleasure of the moment.

It couldn't go on. Blake had shut the door behind him but any moment Jane would be back from picking up the path lab's daily delivery of blood-test results that had just been dropped off at Reception, or someone else would come barging in.

Blake released her and as they faced each other, with eyes locked and their breaths mingling, he said wryly, 'I'm as bad as that teasing colleague of mine, aren't I?'

'So you believe me?'

'Yes, of course I do. But I've just taken advantage of your vulnerability and feelings of indebtedness, haven't I? I suggest we get on with what we're here for, Helena, and it *isn't* romancing around the surgery.'

He was eyeing her whimsically.

'Do you agree?'

She managed a smile.

'Do I have a choice?'

As Jane arrived with the test results at that moment he didn't get the chance to reply, just shook his head and went.

As the other nurse watched him depart, she asked, 'What have you been doing to the male members of the practice? Dr Pemberton has just gone out looking somewhat dazed and Darren has been smirking for most of the afternoon.'

Helena shrugged. It was more a case of what they'd done to her.

Back in his own room Blake was thinking that what had just happened had been inevitable. He and Helena were drawn to each other like magnets. He *did* feel responsible for her.

Didn't want to take advantage of her. But when he'd seen her lying on the couch, gazing up at that blighter Darren, he'd been gripped by such jealousy he'd felt it would choke him.

Yet he should have known better, shouldn't he? If Darren was a flirt, Helena wasn't. But there'd been his awareness of the similarity of their ages. It had made him feel once again as if he came from another planet.

Helena had been right when she'd referred to his monastic existence. He *had* lived on his own too long. But his response had been normal enough when he'd taken her in his arms…and so had hers! She'd been like all his dreams come true when he'd held her, and it had changed everything. It hadn't been to protect and comfort her then.

The force driving him had been desire and he was asking himself where they went from there. He couldn't believe that the fabric of their relationship could shift so quickly. One moment they'd been caring friends. The next in the grip of a passion that was still heating his blood and he knew he was going to have to slow down. He had to give her time, be the sensible one, and it wasn't a role he yearned for.

After he'd finished his solitary evening meal Blake couldn't settle. He had to speak to Helena before the day was out, he told himself. He needed to know what she was thinking of him and there was no way he wanted it to be over the phone.

When she opened the door to him her face was devoid of expression, like a blank page in a book, and his spirits took a downward spiral. He wasn't to know that she'd been having similar thoughts to his. She was in love with him and he'd kissed her for the first time. It had been enchantment, but what had it meant to Blake? He'd soon had his doctor's hat on again, reminding her that there should be no romance in the surgery when she could have stayed in his arms for ever.

'I had to come and see you,' he said quietly, as she stepped back to let him in.

'Why?' she questioned perversely.

'You know why, Helena. Our relationship took a big step forward today.'

'And now you feel it should take a step back?' she said flatly.

'I didn't say that.'

'No, but you're thinking it.'

'I'm thinking that maybe I overstepped the mark. It wasn't what I intended.'

'Thanks for that.'

He ignored the sarcasm. 'For one thing, I'm your employer and for another I let myself get carried away by the after-effects of a searing moment of jealousy. The main thing is, are we still friends?'

She smiled and his spirits lifted. 'Yes, of course we are. How could we be any other after all you've done for me?'

He sighed. 'You are not beholden to me for anything, so will you, please, stop saying those sorts of things? What I did for you I would have done for anyone, so let's wipe the slate clean and start afresh, shall we?'

'Back to how we were before, you mean?'

'Yes.'

'I suppose so,' she agreed meekly, 'if that's how you want it.' She had a vision of the future being a 'matey' sort of place with lots of goodwill and no kisses.

'Goodnight, Helena,' he said softly, and turned to go, knowing that if he stayed a moment longer he would make a mockery of all he'd said by reaching out for her and taking up where they'd left off earlier in the day.

CHAPTER FIVE

A COUPLE of weeks later Blake's contract with the prison service was called upon as it sometimes was. An inmate of a nearby prison had been operated on in a local hospital for a duodenal ulcer and had developed an infection around the partly healed incision.

He had been seen by the prison doctor but, as was often the case, the authorities had called in an unbiased outside practitioner to be involved in the patient's treatment.

Blake found the man in the medical wing of the prison and after examining the infected area he prescribed antibiotics and regular antiseptic swabbing until it healed.

'Doesn't look much of a villain. What's the guy been up to?' he asked a nearby medical orderly.

'Grievous bodily harm on a neighbour,' he was told. 'A fall-out over tall trees blocking out the light. Not a habitual offender and we

124

get plenty of those. We were expecting a real hard man to be transferred here a while back, a gang leader who'd shot a fellow on a garage forecourt, but the authorities changed their minds and sent him further south to a top security prison. He was from the Tyneside area. Kenny Kelsall, the leader of the Kelsall gang.'

Blake felt his insides knotting. They were the people who had terrorised Helena's father. No wonder Kelsall had been sent elsewhere. It would hardly be prudent to have him imprisoned in the same town that James Harris had been moved to.

As he'd driven back to the practice Blake's tension hadn't eased. It wasn't hard to understand why so many people refused to testify in such cases. Thankfully Helena had only been on the edge of the danger. Her father had borne the brunt of it, and now she was rebuilding her life in the best place he could think of to watch over her, the Priory Practice.

Just having her around the place brightened his day. She was keen, efficient and treated the patients with sympathy and understanding. The only person who ever had any criticism to make was Maxine, who was still peeved at the way Blake had produced Helena out of the blue.

Darren was keeping his distance after the episode regarding the consulting-room couch, and as for Helena herself she was keeping a low profile with them all, especially himself, he thought ruefully.

But who was to blame for that? He was. He'd made such a fuss about the incident and had then fallen over himself to give her the impression that he deeply regretted having given in to a longing that she knew nothing about.

So was it any wonder that she was friendly but distant? What would she say, he wondered, if she knew that it took all his willpower not to go round to the cottage in the evenings? But he'd vowed to give her time. Time to adjust to a new job, a new home and a new man who for the first time in three years was attracted to another woman.

There was no way he was going to tell her what he'd heard back there in the prison. It was the last thing she would want to hear. The witness protection programme was in the past and that was where she would want it to stay.

The waiting room was full when he got back and amongst those waiting to see him were a pair of young newly-weds. They'd asked for genetic testing because there was a history of haemophilia in the girl's family and she wanted to know if she was a carrier.

He'd passed them on to the appropriate departments and now they had come for the results of the tests that had been done. She was tense and anxious as they faced him and Blake felt that what he had to impart was going to be seen as a mixture of good news and bad.

'You don't carry the haemophilia gene,' he told her, 'but you have got another genetic disorder that has similar overtones.'

'What is it?' she asked in a low voice.

'Von Willebrand's disease. I suspected it when you said that your gums bleed easily, you have frequent nosebleeds and heavy periods, all symptoms of the illness. It's from a defective gene, like a lot of genetic disorders, but unlike haemophilia it affects both the sexes equally. Those who have it suffer from a lack of substance in their blood called the von Willebrand factor which plays a vital role in the clotting process. It's hereditary, but this illness is not from the combination of two faulty genes, it comes from just the one. There is no cure, I'm afraid, but it can be treated.' Blake explained more about the illness and its treatment. He also gave them information about support groups and made arrangements for the couple to have genetic counselling, as they had asked about the chances of passing von Willebrand's on to a child.

'The young couple that have been to see you looked very sad when they were leaving,' Helena said when surgery was over and she found him on his own in the kitchen having a quick coffee. 'She was weeping.'

He nodded sombrely. 'With good reason, I'm afraid. I'd just had to tell her that she hadn't got the genetic illness she thought she had, but that she's got something almost as distressing and as it's inherited she could pass it on to their children.'

'Health care is a mixture of misery and happiness,' Helena said solemnly. 'Misery for those who can't be cured and happiness for those who can, and for those of us with good health it's a gift to treasure.'

He was smiling. 'You're very philosophical this morning.'

It was the first time he'd seen her since getting back from the prison and now the memory of what the prison nurse had said was back. Hopefully Helena would never know that Kelsall had almost been on their doorstep.

In the short time they'd known each other there had been enough spectres in her life. Her terror the night when the white van had been parked at the back of the cottage had been proof enough of the state she was in.

But now, hopefully for Helena, it was all over. She was settling in at the practice, liked living in the cottage and they had a pleasant, peaceful relationship that he was just about coping with.

She was watching him with the bright gaze that was so much a part of her these days and as if she was reading his mind she asked, 'What are you thinking about? The prison?'

'No, of course not,' he lied. 'I was thinking that you're a changed person.'

She was laughing and as he watched her lips draw back over even white teeth Blake knew he wanted to kiss her again, to feel her slender suppleness hard up against him. It was all right, this 'good friends' routine, but it didn't banish the longing that kept him awake at night and filled his days with maybes.

'Changed for the better, I hope,' she teased.

'Of course. It goes without saying.'

She could have told him that he wasn't wrong. She *had* changed, but not in the way *he* meant. She'd changed from being footloose and fancy-free to a woman in love with her boss, and how long she could exist without telling him so she didn't know.

But once again they were in a situation where they could be interrupted at any moment and on impulse she said, 'Are you doing anything tonight?'

She watched dark brows rise in surprise and held her breath.

'Er…no. Nothing special anyway. Why do you ask?'

'I thought I could cook you a meal. My skills are somewhat basic, but it would be one way of saying thank you.'

Blake frowned. 'I thought we'd decided that the grateful scenario was in the past.'

She sighed. 'All right, then. If I'm not allowed to be grateful...will you come because I want to get to know you better? I know Dr Pemberton of the Priory Practice, the police surgeon and the prison practitioner. I also know the good neighbour. Oops! Sorry for bringing that up again. But I don't really know the man beneath all those guises and I'd like to know him better.'

The brows were still raised.

'You would?'

'Yes. I would.'

'You might be disappointed.'

She could hear footsteps outside the kitchen and said in a low voice, 'I'll be the judge of that. So will you come...about eightish?'

'Yes. I'll come,' he said, and went striding back to his own sanctum with the feeling that a very interesting evening lay ahead.

As soon as she'd issued the invitation Helena began to have doubts. Would Blake guess there was a motive behind it, and what would she give him to eat? There were three things in her repertoire—casserole, grilled steak and boiled eggs.

Obviously she couldn't give the man in her life a boiled egg after a hard day's work. A casserole took ages and was hardly original, so fillet steak and mushrooms it was going to have to be, and some quick shopping was called for the moment she went off duty.

'You look preoccupied,' Jane said in the middle of the afternoon. 'Is everything all right?'

'Er…yes,' Helena told her. 'It's just that I'm having someone round for a meal and my cooking skills are limited. I've spent most of my working life eating in hospital staff restaurants and when I haven't been working I've eaten out or bought a take-away.'

'Don't try to be too clever,' Jane said. 'Do whatever you do best for the main course and buy something for dessert. With a bottle of wine to wash it down you can't go wrong. May I ask who you're entertaining?'

Helena smiled. 'You can ask, yes. But it doesn't mean I'm going to tell you.'

'Someone from here?'

'Maybe.'

'Dr Scott?'

'No.'

'Dr Fielding?'

'No.'

'Then it has to be Dr Pemberton. As if I didn't know.'

'I just want to make a gesture after all he's done for me.'

'Sure,' Jane agreed with a smile of her own, 'and did he take much persuading? We *are* talking about a man whose social life is somewhat restricted...by choice. For instance, I know one person who would jump through a hoop if it would mean him looking in her direction, but Blake has more sense than that.'

'You mean Maxine?'

'I do indeed. She's a good doctor, but waspish with it, and wasn't too pleased when Blake pulled *you* out of the hat.'

There'd been patients to see to and the conversation had ended there but as Helena buzzed around the supermarket after work she was remembering it. Was it so obvious that she was in love with Blake? she wondered. She hoped not.

He'd already made it clear that he didn't want her to keep expressing her thanks. So how would he react if he discovered that her feelings went a lot deeper than that? Since the day they'd kissed he'd never touched her, and she didn't know if it was because she no longer aroused any feelings in him or if he didn't approve of relationships within the practice. Or maybe there was some other reason.

She wished she knew. But maybe tonight the answer would present itself. Just the two of them alone in the cosy cottage. She intended to look her best, and once she'd prepared the food she went for a leisurely soak.

Helena often wore green. It was her favourite colour, matching her eyes and enhancing her hair. Tonight she was torn between a soft green top with tight cream trousers and a dress of the same colour that clung to her hips and the firm globes of her breasts. It was low cut and flattering, but would Blake be expecting her to dress up to such an extent for a meal on a weekday evening?

If there was any chance of their relationship moving on while they were in each other's company, she didn't want it to be because he thought she was sending out signals and so the dress went back into the wardrobe.

She'd explored the cupboards of the rented house and had found some reasonable china, glassware and cutlery, and as she set the table her hands weren't quite steady. Was she taking too much upon herself, she wondered, trying to make a confirmed widower fall in love with her? Blake must have met heaps of women since he'd lost his wife but none of them had been given the chance to fill the gap in his life, so why did she think it would be any different with her?

When she heard his ring on the doorbell just after eight, the table was lit by candles, the vegetables were simmering on the stove, the steak was ready to go under the grill and the wine uncorked. A quick glance in the mirror told her that she was looking good and with a serene smile she went to greet him.

But if she was feeling at peace with the world, Blake wasn't. He was frowning.

'I'm afraid I can't stay, Helena,' he said. 'The police phoned while I was on the way here. There's been a body found in the grounds of a hotel not far from here.'

'No!' she wailed. 'Can't they get someone else to go?'

He shook his head.

'Afraid not. I'm not the only police surgeon in the area but I'm the only one available at this moment. I'll deal with it as quickly as I can, but can't guarantee how long it will take. I never know what I'm going to find on these occasions.'

As the evening stretched ahead without him she said, 'Can't I go with you? It would be better than waiting here.'

'Are you sure you want to?' he asked in surprise. 'It could be grim…and I would have thought that any sort of crime scene wouldn't be your idea of pleasure after what has happened recently.'

'This is different, though, isn't it?' she persisted. 'It's not connected with me. I would stay in the background while you were doing what you have to.'

She could have told him that the pleasure of it would be being in his company. The rest of it she would ignore.

'All right, then,' he conceded. 'Make sure you switch everything off before we go so that we don't return to burnt offerings.' As she obeyed he got back into the car and waited for her to join him.

'I'm really sorry about this,' he said as he pulled out on to the road. 'It's one of the drawbacks of working with the police, never knowing when I'll be needed. Normally it doesn't bother me. The work is challenging and rewarding, but on occasions such as this I could do without it.'

Helena smiled across at him and he thought that she was blossoming before his eyes, this nurse who was never out of his thoughts. He liked everything about her. The spirit that was beginning to show through after her awful homecoming. The way she was coping with having had her life turned upside down and finding herself amongst strangers. Her efficient approach to the job. He could go on for ever.

She was beautiful in a fresh, natural sort of way and incredibly was asking for the chance to get to know him better, he thought as his pulses leapt. But was she going to be disappointed? He'd had all the stuffing knocked out of him when he'd lost Anna and Jason, and ever since it had seemed a safe option to stay single. That way he wasn't likely to have to face heartbreak again.

Bringing his mind back to lighter things, he said whimsically, 'So what sort of a feast am I missing?'

Helena laughed. 'If we ever get around to it, back to basics is a better description than a feast. I do a much-admired boiled egg, a haphazard sort of casserole that was once described as a gastronomic mystery tour and have been known to do a reasonable grilled steak.'

'And which of those delights did you decide upon?'

'The steak.'

He gave an exaggerated sigh of relief.

'It would seem the best choice.'

'I suppose that you are up to cordon bleu standard,' she teased, 'if your cooking is as exemplary as everything else you do.'

'Let's just say that I've got a good tin opener,' he quipped back, and as the hotel they were heading for came into view at that moment the seriousness of what they were about to be involved in took over.

A woman's body lay spread-eagled on the paved walkway almost directly beneath the balcony of a fourth-floor bedroom at the back of the hotel.

'A gardener found her,' a police sergeant told him. 'It looks as if she either lost her balance, threw herself over or someone else did. Nobody heard anything, but the receptionist said that the woman had lost her voice, laryngitis or something similar. And added to that, none of the rooms at the back here are occupied, except for the one she was in.'

Helena had moved to one side so as not to be in the way as Blake lifted the tape that the police had used to keep the public back, but she could see the extent of the victim's injuries and they were severe. She was lying face down with her limbs bent grotesquely, and the back of her head was covered in blood.

'The DCI's on the phone, wanting a word with you, Sarge,' a young constable said as Blake began a careful examination of the dead woman. 'They've identified her from the information found in the hotel room, and for some reason he's going spare.'

The woman had hit the ground face down, which made Blake think that the injuries to the back of her head were from a blow rather than the fall, indicating some sort of foul play. There was no pulse or heartbeat, but the body was still warm so it hadn't been all that long ago since she'd fallen.

As he got slowly to his feet the sergeant was back and his face was grim.

'It appears the victim flew in from Spain this morning to give evidence for the prosecution at a big drugs trial. She'd been booked into this place and was going to be under police surveillance until she flew back in a couple of days. But it looks as if she was got at. We were told she was coming in on an evening flight, but she must have come earlier, which makes it look as if somebody knew more than we did.'

Blake's glance was on Helena, sitting on a garden bench that was thankfully out of earshot. The last thing he wanted was for her to hear that this woman had been killed because she had been prepared to be a witness in a court case. Helena's father's ordeal was behind her now, but it didn't stop him from feeling that it would do her no good to hear about anything else of that nature after what she'd gone through.

Twice in one day he'd been on the fringe of gangland matters. Thank goodness it was nothing to do with the Kelsalls. That name was beginning to haunt him. But Kenny was under lock and key somewhere down south and the rest of his gang were still involved in the crime scene going around Newcastle.

But it didn't alter the fact that Helena's life had been touched by them and if the fates had been less kind they might have got to know of her existence, sought her out, and it could have been her lying there.

She was looking over at him and gave him a brief smile, and he thought dismally that this would have to happen just when they'd planned to spend some time together. What she didn't know about she wouldn't worry about, but it had certainly put the blight on his evening…

'Forensics will have to check out the injuries to the back of the head,' he told the policeman soberly. 'I don't think they came from the fall, but they're the best people to look into that.'

He took a deep breath. 'What will happen now in the court case? Was she the only witness?'

The sergeant shrugged. 'Seems like it. They'll probably postpone the trial, or let him go free through lack of evidence.'

When he rejoined her, Helena said, 'What's wrong, Blake? Was it bad?'

He shook his head. 'No. I've seen a lot worse. But the value that some people put on human life sickens me.'

'So it wasn't an accident?'

'I don't think so. I think the woman was hit on the back of the head and then pushed over the balcony, but it's for the police and forensics to sort that out.'

He was conscious that his voice sounded harsh, but he couldn't help it. If he hadn't been involved in working with the police neither of them would have been caught up in tonight's incident. And yet if he hadn't been a police surgeon he would never have met Helena, which did tilt the scales somewhat.

And now he just wanted to get her away from there and back to the untainted atmosphere of the cottage.

He couldn't care less if they ate or not. He'd lost his appetite. So much for the pleasant evening he'd been looking forward to. It had been gruesome and unsettling and had left him on edge.

'Come on, Helena,' he said abruptly. 'Let's go. Tonight has been one of the times when I wish I wasn't a police surgeon.'

Back at the cottage she sat him down with a drink in the small sitting room and went to start afresh on the meal.

'The vegetables have gone all mushy,' she told him, standing in the doorway with a saucepan in each hand. 'I hope you don't mind.'

Blake didn't answer. He was gazing into space, with eyes narrowed and jaw tight. Something had happened out there in the grounds of the hotel, she thought. But what? Surely he'd seen enough of that sort of thing for it not to get to him, but for some reason tonight's incident had done so and she would like to know why.

'She wasn't someone you knew, like it was with my dad, was she?' she asked, and that brought him back on line.

'No, of course not,' he said with a tight smile. 'Let's forget it, shall we? And, no, I don't mind the vegetables being soggy. I'm fastening my hopes on the steak.'

It wasn't true. He still felt as if food would choke him. The only good thing about the bizarre episode was that she hadn't heard what the policeman had said, so if it had brought his nightmares back, at least she'd been spared a recurrence of hers, and he was determined that was how it was going to stay.

He would have to eat. Helena was geared up for the meal and he couldn't disappoint her, though what sort of company he was going to be in his state of mind he didn't know.

It was uncanny. On two occasions in recent weeks something strange had happened when he'd been called out by the police. He'd seen plenty of corpses in his time as his duties covered a fair-sized area, but nothing like this. First of all there'd been her father, who had turned out to be his next-door neighbour, and it looked as if tonight's victim had been caught up in a similar situation.

When Helena announced that the meal was ready he got up slowly and followed her into the dining room without speaking. She was observing him reproachfully.

'I don't care what you say, Blake,' she told him. 'Something *is* wrong. If it's because your call-out interrupted the evening, forget it.' Her lip trembled. 'Or are you looking for an excuse to go? Maybe you're having second thoughts about us. If you are, feel free. The last thing I want is for you to be here against your will.

Perhaps you were glad of the interruption and are now wishing it had lasted longer.'

'You're talking rubbish, Helena,' he growled. 'Of course I want to be here.'

'So perhaps you could look as if you do,' she flashed back angrily. 'Because if this is how you look when you want to be with me, I wouldn't like to see you when you don't.'

'You don't understand,' he said in the same tone. 'I have things on my mind.'

'Fair enough. and are you going to tell me what they are?'

He shook his head. 'No. I'm going to eat the meal that you've so kindly prepared and then I'm leaving. The evening got off to a bad beginning. I think we ought to forget it and start again. That business at the hotel did take the edge off it, I must admit.' And if that wasn't a prize understatement he didn't know what was.

When they'd finished eating he did as he'd said, got up to go, and for the first time since their exchange of words their glances held.

'I know I've been a pain tonight, Helena,' he said stiffly. 'All I can say is that I've had my reasons. They are connected with you, but not in the way you think. By the next time we meet I will have adjusted, but for the moment I'm not thinking very straight.'

'Are you trying to tell me that getting to know me better would conflict with your memories of your family?' she asked slowly, and watched his face stretch.

Then it was her turn to be surprised as he replied, 'No. I accept that they are gone for ever. It has nothing to do with that.'

At the door he kissed her gently on the brow and she could have wept. What had happened to all her high hopes, her plans for a romantic evening? They'd disappeared with the finding of that poor woman's body, and she wished she understood why.

'Lock up after I've gone,' he told her sombrely, 'and make sure that you switch on the security lights and activate the burglar alarm.'

'I always do,' she told him flatly, and as he walked down the path to his car it took all her strength of will not to run after him and beg him to come back.

*   *   *

As Blake drove home his face was grim. What a fiasco the evening had turned out to be. He'd set off for the cottage at eight o'clock in a buoyant mood and had been only mildly miffed when the call had come from the police station, thinking that it was all part of a day's work and would soon be sorted.

Helena wanting to go with him had been a surprise but, keen for her company, he'd agreed, never dreaming that he was going to hear something that would horrify and sicken him.

Her own nightmare was in the past. He kept telling himself that and knew it to be true. But it didn't take away the feeling of nausea or lessen the determination that from now on he was going to see that she kept out of danger and had no connection in any way with the seedy side of life.

She must have thought him a complete idiot the way he'd behaved when they'd got back to the cottage, he told himself as he garaged the car. It took a lot to throw him into that state, but he was in love with her, wasn't he? Wanted to spend the rest of his life with her.

He'd already lost one woman he loved. If the precious gift of another deep commitment was to come his way, he would protect and cherish her with every fibre of his being and pray that Helena would never again be tainted by the wrongdoing of others.

CHAPTER SIX

'So how did it go?' Jane asked the next morning as the two nurses were preparing for the day ahead.

'Don't ask,' Helena told her ruefully. 'Blake was called out by the police on his way to the cottage so that had to come first, which wasn't really a problem. He let me go with him and I just sat around until he'd done what he had to do.'

'Which was?'

'There'd been a suspicious death at a hotel. A woman had fallen from a fourth-floor balcony and been killed. He seemed to think she'd been hit before she fell and once he'd pronounced her dead he left it to the police and we were able to depart.'

'So what was the problem?'

'He was. When we got back to the cottage he was all silent and peculiar but wouldn't tell me why. I think he was regretting us meeting outside working hours. Not wanting to break the fast maybe. He insisted it wasn't that, but there was definitely something on his mind, and after we'd eaten he went. So the whole thing was a big flop.'

'I can't believe that he didn't want to be with you,' Jane remarked thoughtfully. 'I've seen the way he looks at you. You are just what he needs, Helena. Someone young, beautiful and kind, who will give him other children. Blake has been without someone to cherish him for too long.'

Helena sighed. 'Maybe, but after last night's performance I don't think it's going to be me.'

'Time will tell,' the other nurse said comfortingly.

'Yes, I'm sure it will,' Helena agreed flatly, as she watched Blake's car pull up outside the practice.

What would he have to say today? she wondered. Would he have an explanation for last night? His behaviour had been totally out of character from what she'd seen of him so far. Maybe he was the type of person who went into sudden depressions and that had been her first experience of it. There were people like that. She'd met them in hospitals and clinics and knew that the black clouds could come from nowhere.

If that *had* been the case there was no sign of it this morning, she thought as he came striding into the nurses' room a few moments later, his usual brisk and energetic self.

'Good morning, Jane, Helena,' he said pleasantly, but she noticed that he looked away the moment his glance met hers. Annoyance was beginning to uncurl inside her. The man last night hadn't been the Blake she knew and the one with the evasive smile this morning wasn't either. What was going on? She deserved to know.

Yet there was no way she was going to insist on it. She'd asked him what was wrong often enough last night, and now it was up to Blake to put things right between them. If he was going to behave as if nothing had happened, he wasn't the man she'd thought he was.

As the day progressed they were both kept busy but Helena knew that he could have found the time for a quick word if he'd so desired. But it seemed as if he must have a short memory, or else he was thinking that least said, soonest mended.

Perhaps she was making too big a fuss. It didn't mean that because she'd invited him round for a meal he had to be grovelling at her feet because he hadn't been the life and soul of the party.

If he'd felt tired or out of sorts he could have said so and she wouldn't have minded, but she sensed that it was more than that. He'd been fine until the moment they'd arrived at the hotel and he'd seen the body.

Surely it wasn't someone he knew, as had been the case with her father, and he wasn't saying. There'd been nothing to indicate that had been the case. Blake had just looked grim and white-faced when he'd told her he was finished there and she'd thought there was nothing strange about that. In both his commitment to the police and the prison service he would be used to distressing situations and last night's incident would have been worse than some and better than others.

Jane went home early as her husband wasn't well and there was only Helena in the nurses' room when Blake looked in at the end of the day. It was the opportunity he'd been waiting for and, shutting the door behind him, he said, 'Are you doing anything tonight?'

'Why?' she asked tartly. 'I hope you're not going to suggest a chat. It would seem a bit inopportune after last night's big silence, don't you think? Though I do feel you owe me an explanation.'

She was used to seeing a friendly sort of affection in his glance when he looked at her, but the dark eyes meeting hers, squarely this time, were unreadable, as if he'd drawn a curtain over what was in his mind.

He *did* owe her an explanation, Blake was thinking, but it wasn't going to be the truth and that was going against the grain. He wasn't in the habit of lying, but he felt it was for the best. Through his job as police surgeon he'd had another opportunity to see what a frightening place the criminal underworld was and all he wanted to do was protect Helena from it.

It wasn't touching them any more, but it didn't make it any the less worrying that such goings-on were still happening, and if she were to find out it would destroy her new-found feeling of security. So an untruth it was going to be.

'I had a migraine,' he told her. 'A really bad one. And the best thing seemed to be for me to go home to bed.'

'Without telling me why?' she questioned incredulously. 'I *am* a nurse! And it's taken all day for you to tell me *that*.'

'Yes. I *do* know that you're a nurse,' he said patiently, as if she lacked comprehension. 'But *I'm* a doctor and we doctors are supposed to heal ourselves, rather than burdening others with our aches and pains.'

Helena sighed. She didn't believe him. Blake was fobbing her off. But it seemed there was no use arguing about it. He'd ruined the evening she'd planned and wasn't going to say why, so there wasn't much she could do about it.

If he really had felt unwell, he had her sympathy, but she was in love with him. His every expression, word, deed were engraved on her heart. The Blake she knew would have told her he wasn't well and done something about it, instead of sitting sombre and unspeaking.

'So why do you want to see me tonight?' she asked perversely. 'You've explained what was wrong, which doesn't leave much else to say.'

He smiled and that made her feel even more fractious.

'We've never been short of something to talk about before,' he protested mildly, 'but you are determined to make me squirm, aren't you? It was only one night of our lives that was upset. It's not as if we were never going to see each other again.'

He was right, of course, she thought penitently. She was making a huge fuss about nothing and she managed a smile of her own.

'I'm sorry for acting like a child that's had a toy taken from it, Blake,' she told him. 'You must think me very infantile. I suppose it's because I was so looking forward to it. But, as you say, there will be other nights.'

'Like tonight, for instance. Let's go for a drive and stop off for a drink somewhere,' he suggested.

'Yes, all right,' she agreed, thinking wryly that being on her high horse hadn't lasted long.

'So I'll pick you up about seven?'

'Yes.'

They had left the town behind and were driving through small villages where stone-built cottages with pretty gardens were scattered against a backdrop of green meadows when Blake said, 'My life is not as ''womanless'' as you might think. I'm going to take you to meet a very special lady.'

Helena stared at him. He hadn't said anything about visiting someone. Was that what had been behind him suggesting that they go for a drive, to introduce her to a woman friend that she hadn't known existed?

They'd chatted about this and that ever since he'd picked her up, both of them determined to keep it light, but what Blake had just said changed all that. For one thing it showed that he hadn't forgotten she'd described him as womanless, and for another, why should he want her to meet some strange woman, unless maybe he had a message he wanted to get across?

Perhaps therein lay the true answer to last night's moodiness. He'd felt she was coming on to him too strongly and thought he'd better put her in the picture.

While the thoughts were whizzing round in her mind Blake pulled up outside what looked like a converted manor house, and Helena's eyes widened.

His woman friend was obviously a few steps higher in the social strata than an orphaned nurse without a relative in the world.

He went round to her side of the car and stood beside the open door, waiting for her to get out.

'You'll like Rowena,' he said as she swivelled round to stand beside him.

I doubt it, she thought glumly.

There was the warmth of a deep affection in his voice and her spirits were plummeting fast. This was planned, she thought. Blake had brought her to see his woman friend to clear

the air. This meeting *was* going to be the answer to his strange mood of the night before.
Because he was kind, he was telling her this
way that she was presuming too much. It
would save them both embarrassment.

He was observing her quizzically.

'Are you rooted to the spot or something?'
he asked mildly, as if he hadn't a clue to what
must be going on in her mind.

Helena pulled herself together and flashed
him a smile that was more of a grimace than
a beam.

'No, of course not. Lead on,' she said quietly, praying that she would be able to come
out of this meeting with some dignity left.

An elderly housekeeper type of person
opened the door to them and her face lit up
when she saw Blake.

'Dr Pemberton!' she said. 'Do come in.'

'Hello, Mrs Porteous,' he said. 'I've brought
a friend of mine to meet Rowena.'

Still smiling, the woman said, 'You will
both be most welcome. Madam is in the sitting
room.'

Helena was looking around her. Everything about the house and its contents spoke of wealth and good taste. She could visualise Blake living here. The house had class and so had he. And, no doubt, so had Rowena.

The woman gazing through the window was elegant, white-haired and frail. She was sitting in a wheelchair and Helena thought that it would seem that she was meeting the mother before the daughter, but she felt her face go slack as Blake walked swiftly across thick carpeting and said gently, 'Hello, Rowena. How are you?'

'All the better for seeing you, my dear,' she said warmly. Bright blue eyes looked in Helena's direction. 'And who is this that you have brought to see me?'

Blake took Helena's hand and drew her forward.

'Helena is our new practice nurse. She has recently come to live in the area and is only just getting to know the place and its people.'

'And what better person to take you under his wing than Blake,' the woman in the wheelchair said. 'He was there for me when I needed someone and has been my friend ever since. Now, do sit down, both of you, and I'll ask Mrs Porteous to make a pot of tea.'

Helena was only too glad to deposit herself onto the nearest chair. She was light-headed with relief. Yet shouldn't she have known better? Blake wasn't the sort of man for playing mind games and manipulating people.

He was eyeing her questioningly, sensing the chaos of her thoughts, and as the mouth that was made for his kisses curved into a smile he relaxed. Whatever it was that had been bothering Helena, it had obviously resolved itself, he thought. And he'd dearly wanted her to meet Rowena.

All three of them had known sorrow. The frail woman sitting by the window hadn't wanted to live when he'd first met her, and it had been in helping her that he had found some ease for his own pain.

'So, tell me about yourself, Helena,' Rowena Maddox said, as they drank tea out of china cups and ate little fairy cakes. 'Where do you come from?'

Helena swallowed hard. It was hardly likely that this charming woman had any friends amongst local criminals, but she was always going to be careful about what she said to anyone other than Blake. So she told her, 'I'm from up north'.

'I would have known from your accent,' Rowena said, 'and so why so far away from home?'

'My father, who died recently, wanted to move to this part of the country, and as I was overseas at the time it didn't really register with me. But since I've been back I'm having to get used to a different lifestyle.'

'So you aren't intending going back to where you came from?'

Helena's glance was on Blake as she shook her head.

'No. I like it here...very much.'

'Good,' the elderly questioner said firmly, and now her glance was on the dark-eyed doctor who was shaking his head laughingly as if he'd read her thoughts.

*   *   *

'And so who *is* Rowena Maddox?' Helena asked as they drove home through the starlit night.

'She was the sole survivor from the car crash that killed Anna and Jason,' he said sombrely. 'Her husband was driving the other car and he died, too. He had a heart attack at the wheel and crashed into Anna head on. Rowena suffered severe spinal injuries amongst others and has never walked since.

'They phoned me from the hospital to ask if I would go to see her as she had no wish to live, even though she was by then out of Intensive Care. It was the last thing I wanted to do. I had enough of those sorts of feelings of my own to cope with.'

'But you went.'

His smile was grim.

'Yes, I went, and discovered that she was submerged in a pit of guilt. Charles, her husband, was an arrogant type with a serious heart problem. And thought he was above taking medication. He'd missed taking it for days before the accident and every time Rowena thought about Anna and Jason she just wanted to die.'

'How awful.'

'Yes. It was. But it wasn't her fault and I kept telling her so, until finally she began to believe me. Then slowly, oh, so slowly, she regained the will to live.'

'So she was another of your waifs and strays—like me.'

He shook his head. 'No way. Having the extra burden of Rowena's despair to cope with at the time was something I could have done without, but I've been repaid a hundredfold. She gives as well as takes, and during the last three years she's been a wonderful friend, helping me through *my* bad times as I helped her through hers. She's always there for me when I'm feeling low. Between us we've survived, and that was why I wanted you to meet her.'

'I thought she was going to be someone you were in love with. That she was the reason you didn't want to be with me last night.'

He eyed her incredulously. 'You thought that I was going to parade her in front of you to let you see I had other plans?'

'Yes. Something like that.'

His smile was wry. 'Well, you were wrong, weren't you? You must think I place high value on my attractions.'

'I don't think anything of the kind. I just thought you were trying to let me down lightly.'

'And why would I want to do that?'

Here we go! she thought recklessly. The moment has presented itself. Take the bull by the horns.

'Because you know I'm in love with you.'

As his heart leapt in his breast Blake's grip on the steering-wheel tightened. He couldn't keep driving on after that. There was a layby ahead and, slowing down, he pulled into it. Once he'd switched off the engine he turned to her.

'Would you like to say that again?' he said in a low voice.

'Yes, if you want, but I think you heard me the first time. I love you, Blake.'

She noticed he wasn't exactly sweeping her into his arms. Instead, he asked carefully, 'Are you sure you're not confusing love with gratitude? Because that's an emotion you've been experiencing a lot lately.'

'Huh!' she exclaimed, unable to believe that this controlled discussion was taking place after what she'd just told him. 'Can't you credit me with knowing the difference?'

'Yes, I can,' he said gently, 'but I have to be sure. We haven't known each other long, Helena, but as far as I'm concerned every moment since we met has been channelled into a healing process. You're the most beautiful thing I've ever seen. I think about you all the time, but I have a responsibility towards you. I guided you into the life that you now have, and I want to be sure that the time is right for you to make that kind of a decision. You are still vulnerable and it wouldn't be fair of me to take advantage of it. We need to be patient.'

'And that's it!' she cried. 'You're fobbing me off, just like that! How can you? After how I've told you what's in my heart?'

'I can because it seems I have to have the sense for the two of us,' he said levelly. 'But it doesn't mean that I don't want you.'

'Show me, then!'

He reached over and pulled her towards him and with his lips against her hair murmured, 'Every time I look at your mouth I want to kiss it, and the rest of you puts me into a trance of longing.'

'And yet you don't want to hear that I love you.'

'Shush,' he said softly, and then he was doing what he'd said he longed to do and she was kissing him back as if they were about to be parted for ever.

When he let her go Helena collapsed against the back of the seat like a rag doll.

'You can't say you don't love me after that!' she gasped.

'Aren't you rather putting words into my mouth?' he said quizzically, as he switched on the engine.

They were both silent for the rest of the way and when they stopped in front of the cottage

Blake said, 'Don't invite me in, Helena. Or I might want to take up where we left off.'

'And what would be wrong with that?' she asked, with her mouth still warm from his kisses.

'I think we've already gone into it,' he told her, and added, with the previous night's anxieties surfacing, 'Make sure you lock up and put the alarms on.' And on what was becoming to be a regular note of caution he left.

When he'd gone Helena went slowly upstairs to bed. It had been a strange evening, she thought as she absently ran her fingertips along the polished wooden bannister. First there'd been the introduction to Rowena Maddox and the relief that had followed. It had been humbling to see the deep affection between two people who had experienced such tragedy, and it had affected her more so because her own dark days were so recent.

But on the way home different emotions had presented themselves. She'd told Blake that she loved him and he hadn't looked at her in wide-eyed wonder. He'd been cautious one moment and teasing the next.

Yet he'd kissed her as if he'd been promising her something deep and abiding and then, without more ado, had bundled her out of the car, pre-empted any invitation to come inside and brought everything even more down to basics by reminding her to lock up.

So where did they go from there?

The phone rang as Blake was putting his key in the lock and he smiled. It would be one of the two women in his life, he thought. He didn't know which.

It was Rowena, who rarely went to bed before midnight.

'My dear,' she said when they'd exchanged greetings. 'I had to ring. I liked your young nurse. Are you...? Is she...er...?'

'If you're asking if I'm in love with her, the answer is yes, Rowena. At last I've found someone I can care for, but—'

'Oh, don't say there's a but,' she said disappointedly.

'There is, but it's not a big one. Helena has been through a rough time in recent weeks and I've nominated myself as a sort of guardian figure. I'm concerned that she may be mistaking gratitude for love, so for the present I'm not rushing things.'

'I see,' she said. 'But take care that you don't leave it too long, Blake, or someone else might pip you to the post.'

'I'll bear that in mind,' he said, smiling into the receiver. 'And, Rowena...'

'Yes?'

'If I ever get around to popping the question you'll be the first to know and guest of honour at the wedding.'

Her laughter tinkled in his ear and she told him, 'Again, don't leave it too long, my dear. I'm no spring chicken, you know.'

When she'd gone off the line Blake stood with the phone in his hand, gazing into space.

He'd like to know what Helena was thinking at that moment. She was probably wondering what he was up to. One moment he'd been all cool and wary, concealing the elation she'd aroused in him when she'd told him she loved him, and the next he'd thrown caution to the winds and had let desire take over.

As he stripped off for bed he was remembering every moment of it and knew that, though he was normally a patient man, it would take all his willpower to stay away from her until he was satisfied that she was seeing him in the right light.

If Helena had wondered what they would say to each other the next morning she'd had no need to worry. Jane's husband had been rushed into hospital for emergency surgery during the night and Maxine had rung in to say she had a plumbing problem in the shape of a flooded kitchen and was waiting for workmen to arrive. So Helena and Blake were kept extra busy without a moment to spare and up to lunchtime she saw nothing of him.

She knew that he thought her behaviour immature and impulsive and was being careful not to appear so. But it wasn't like that. Everything about him appealed to her. His cool, dark attractiveness, his integrity in all parts of his life…and his kindness. Maybe that most of all.

Only he would have taken time to comfort the woman whose husband's irresponsible behaviour had been the cause of the death of those he loved. Only Blake would have put aside his own affairs and taken time out of his busy life to offer comfort to a desolate stranger that he'd found virtually on his doorstep.

But he didn't want to know, did he? Expressions of gratitude were frowned upon. To him those kinds of things were just part of life, but not as far as everyone was concerned, she thought.

Take the Kelsalls, for instance. They were more interested in killing than kindness and there were plenty more like them. She still shuddered when she thought about how her father had been hounded by them for doing his duty as a good citizen.

It was the diabetes clinic in the afternoon, and while Helena was having a quick bite in the nurses' room before Darren arrived to take over, Blake came in and said, 'So you *are* managing some lunch. Good. With Jane missing I've been hoping you weren't too submerged. Darren and I have just about cleared the waiting room. It's amazing what a differ- ence it makes when one of us is missing.'

'Yes, I can imagine,' she said weakly, with the memory of what had happened in the car the night before so strong in her mind she'd barely heard a word he'd said.

Though it *had* registered that none of it had been personal. But that was about to change.

'Are you all right, Helena?' he asked in a low voice. 'No regrets?'

'It all depends what you're referring to.'

'You know what I'm on about. Last night.'

'If you mean do I regret telling you that I love you? No, I don't regret that,' she said tiredly, pushing a strand of hair off her brow. 'I had all night to think about it and came to the conclusion that you're still not sure about me. Still not sure if you want to risk being hurt again. And young and foolish though you may think I am, I understand that. But, please, don't keep me waiting too long, Blake.'

He took a step towards her and she knew that the moment he touched her she would be lost...again. But if common sense was in short supply, circumstance wasn't. The door opened and Darren came breezing in, and that was the end of that.

'Keep up the good work, Helena,' Blake said blandly, and with a brief nod in his junior partner's direction he went.

'So what was going on, then?' the practice Romeo wanted to know.

'Nothing,' she said coolly, wishing him far away.

As he went through his list of calls for the day Blake was surprised to see that he'd been asked to call at the house next door to his. Was he never to be free of that place? he thought wryly as he headed towards the cul-de-sac that Helena had been so eager to leave.

There were new people in there now. Darren had mentioned that he'd seen in the local paper that it was available for rental furnished, so it would seem that as far as the witness protection people were concerned, it was no longer in use.

He'd seen two young boys kicking a ball around in the garden and a plump woman hanging out washing, but as yet had made no contact. However, it would seem that was about to change.

When he rang the bell the woman he'd seen opened the door looking tired and anxious and the memory of when he'd come to tell Helena that her father was dead came flooding back.

'I'm Dr Pemberton,' he said with a reassuring smile. 'I believe that you sent for me.'

He watched her colour start to rise.

'Er...yes, I did,' she said awkwardly, 'Do come in, Doctor.' She led the way into the sombre sitting room.

'What's the problem?' he asked.

'I keep having panic attacks. That's why I couldn't come to the surgery. I can't face going outside the house. They start with chest pains and pins and needles, and then I begin hyperventilating. It's frightening. The attack only lasts for a few moments but while I'm experiencing it I'm completely helpless.'

'What's going on in your life that could be causing this? Panic attacks are usually stress-related.'

Her smile was wry. 'I'm stressed all right. My husband is the new manager at the bank down the road. We've had to move from the Isle of Wight and what with that, having to get the boys settled into new schools and the house we're buying on a new estate only at the foundations stage, I don't know whether I'm coming or going. I was happy where we were before, which is more than I can say now. I don't know anyone here and I'm lonely, in spite of having my family around me.'

'I'm your next-door neighbour,' he told her, 'so at least now you know me, and if you need any help with anything at all, don't be afraid to ask.'

Her face brightened. 'You live next door! That makes me feel better already. I feel a fraud as I'm perfectly all right at the moment, but I had an attack this morning and my husband, who thinks he is the only one under pressure, insisted I send for you.'

'Don't worry about having me here under false pretences,' he told her. 'If it occurs again put a small paper bag over your nose and mouth and breathe into it for a few minutes. That should relieve the hyperventilation and the rest will subside with it. There are relaxation classes you could attend if you so wish.'

She gave a nervous smile.

'I'll try the paper bag method first, I think.'

'Certainly,' he agreed, 'but do try to relax. Once you've settled in properly and your stress level is reduced, the attacks should ease off.'

As he continued on his rounds Blake debated whether he should tell Helena about the new people in the house next door. Jean and Joe McIntosh or their sons might have cause to visit the surgery and it could give her a jolt when she saw the address. He was picking and choosing what he felt she should know and had a feeling that it wouldn't go down too well if Helena found out.

'There are some new people in the house next to me,' he said when he got back and found her alone after the diabetes clinic had finished. 'I thought I'd better mention it in case you came across them here at the practice and saw the address.'

He watched her face whiten.

'Poor things,' she said.

'No, it's not like that, Helena. It's the new bank manager and his family. They're nothing to do with the witness protection programme. They're renting it until their new house is ready.'

Her face lit up.

'Wonderful! But why did they call you out?'

'The lady of the house is having panic attacks due to the stress of moving and finding new schools for the children and so on. And it's not the most cheerful of properties, is it?'

'Far from it,' she agreed with feeling.

CHAPTER SEVEN

AUTUMN was taking the place of summer's light evenings and mornings and Helena was regretful that the golden days during which she'd first met Blake were drawing to a close.

Yet she knew she shouldn't be. She needed to be grateful that she'd been given the chance to get to know him. They'd moved on a lot since the morning of her father's death and their relationship would progress even further if he would stop holding back.

But whatever happened between them in the future she would still have the pleasure of working alongside him at the practice. That wasn't going to change, and she wished that the rest of what was going on in their lives was as certain.

Blake was as caring and considerate as ever, but that was it. If she was seeing a lot of him during the daytime it wasn't so in the evenings. He rarely called round at the cottage and if he did, he didn't stay long.

She had decided that any more forward moves had to come from him. He knew what her feelings were. She'd made it plain enough, but he was obviously putting the brakes on where his were concerned.

He was busy, of course, as always, taking his turn to man the clinic at the prison for the benefit of sick inmates needing the care of a GP, dealing with call-outs from the police and pulling his weight at the practice into the bargain.

They did talk sometimes, but it was usually about everyday things. She asked him once about the family living next door to him and he said, 'They seem to be blending in all right among the other people in the cul-de-sac, which I'm sure is what Jean McIntosh wants. Her husband has his new job to keep him occupied and if it's a promotion, as it usually is in these instances, he'll be engrossed in proving himself, while she is left to see to the basics.'

'I wonder what she'd say if she knew what the house had been used for previously,' Helena said pensively.

'I don't think she'd be very happy,' he replied, 'but don't forget they are only temporary occupants.'

He thought afterwards that no one would have lived there for a shorter time than Helena. He only had to look at the place and it brought it all back. But if *he* couldn't get away from it, at least *she* was free from the constant reminder, tucked away in the cottage. It was one of the reasons why he'd never invited her back to his house since those first traumatic days after their meeting...

If he'd met her under normal circumstances he wouldn't be holding back. He would have kissed the breath out of her when she'd said she loved him and had a ring on her finger before she could blink. But as well as the circumstances of their meeting, there was his widower status to consider. He had to be sure that he was ready to take the step that might lead to heartache as much as happiness. He didn't want Helena to have to cope with a man who couldn't let go of the past. She deserved better than that.

One evening after Helena had been to see Jane's husband, who was now recovering after surgery, a chauffeur-driven Daimler pulled up beside her in the gathering dusk. As she looked at it in surprise the window was wound down and she found Rowena observing her smilingly from inside its luxurious interior.

'Helena!' she said. 'It is you, isn't it?' When Helena nodded, she went on, 'I thought it was. I'm so glad I've seen you. Did you know that it's Blake's birthday on Saturday? I wondered if you'd both like to come for a meal.'

Helena hesitated. She didn't know what to say. Blake might not want to take her. He might prefer to dine with Rowena alone.

'It's very kind of you to suggest it,' she said uncomfortably, 'but maybe you'd better ask him first.'

Rowena got the message. 'Yes, all right, I'll do that, but I really would like to meet you again. Can I give you a lift?' she asked.

'I'm only a matter of yards from my front door,' Helena told her. 'But thanks for the offer.'

As the big car pulled away into the night she found herself smiling. If she hadn't seen Rowena she wouldn't have known that Saturday was a special day. Would Blake want her to dine with him at Rowena's, though?

'I saw Rowena last night,' she told him, the following morning.

He was opening the mail and looked up briefly.

'Yes, she rang me afterwards. Where had you been?'

Helena stared at him. Why the sudden interest? *He* didn't want to share her evenings, so why ask.

Blake could tell what was going through her mind, but it didn't mean that because he kept away he didn't think about her all the time. In fact, he was beginning to feel that he was crazy, denying himself when there was no need.

'I'd been to see Jane's husband, when Rowena's car pulled up beside me.'

'Yes. She says she wants us to dine with her on Saturday. Are you free, Helena?'

'Yes, of course, I'm free,' she replied flatly. 'What else would I be doing?'

Her Saturdays of late had been made up of shopping, an early meal, followed by the first showing at one of the town cinemas and then home to bed.

'So you'll go with me?'

'Yes, of course. I'd love to,' she said, perking up by the moment, but she couldn't resist saying, 'What do you see it as? A chance to build bridges, or mend them perhaps?'

'What are you on about?' he said with dry amusement. 'I would say that communications between us are rock solid.'

'Huh! As far as you're concerned, maybe. *I've* told you exactly how *I* feel, which gives *you* the advantage as you're not very forthcoming about your own feelings.'

'How many times do I have to tell you that all I'm asking for is patience on your part?'

'I would have said that you already have it, which just goes to show how ''rock solid'' our communications are. I could go back home to live now that I'm free of the situation Dad was pushed into. All my friends are there, but instead I'm wandering around in a strange place like a lost soul, all because I can't bear to be away from you.'

'Come here, Helena,' he said softly, beckoning her across the room. When she went to stand beside him he took her hands in his, knowing that once again they were in the surgery, which was the worst possible place for serious talking.

'I didn't know you were homesick,' he said in a low voice. 'You never said so. Have I bulldozed you into staying in this place when you'd rather be somewhere else?'

She sighed. 'Of course not. Haven't I just told you why I don't want to leave here?'

'And I'm flattered, but...'

'I know what you're going to say. *I've* got to be sure. *You've* got to be sure. I thought falling in love was supposed to be heady and exciting.'

His hold on her tightened. 'It is, but it's also about caring and sharing, putting the other one first. From what you've told me you've never had a serious relationship and it's a different dimension altogether compared to flirting around.'

'Thanks for the vote of confidence,' she said coolly. 'It's nice to know that you think me incapable of any deep feelings.'

'I don't remember saying that.'

She was drawing away from him. 'Let's just look forward to Saturday and forget the rest. I'm sure you'll feel that's a suggestion in keeping with my butterfly mind.' And before he could argue she'd gone bustling back to her own domain and the patients who were slowly filling up the waiting room.

On Saturday afternoon Helena went shopping for a birthday gift for Blake. It was the first chance she'd had and would be the last as she would be giving it to him that evening.

She would dearly have liked to have bought him a ring but had already scrapped the idea, feeling that it might be seen as too presumptuous. But she still ended up in a prestigious jeweller's in the town centre, searching for a tasteful frame for the photograph she'd just had taken at a fast print shop.

Maybe always having her face in front of him would make Blake forget all the pros and cons, she thought wickedly when she'd found what she wanted. It was after she'd paid for it and was about to leave the shop that the pleasant afternoon became a nightmare.

As she was going through the door three men with faces covered pushed past her. One of them lunged towards her but she pushed him away and flung herself through the door and onto the pavement outside, only to come face to face with a fourth man who was trying to catch up with the others and cover his face at the same time.

It was a strange and frightening moment and would have been more so if he'd been armed, but just the sight of him was enough to send her running in the opposite direction, though not before she'd had a good look at his face.

As she fled past the shop window Helena could see the men smashing glass cases and grabbing handfuls of jewellery, while the shop assistants and a couple of customers lay face down on the floor.

'Ring the police!' she told the startled owner of the menswear shop next door. 'The jeweller's is being robbed!' As he scurried to obey she ran to stand in the shadows by the door.

The robbers were leaving. A van was pulling up outside and the thieves were flinging themselves and their booty into it.

When they'd gone she ran back into the shop and saw that the manager was gazing around him in stunned disbelief, one of the women assistants had fainted and the rest were slowly getting to their feet.

Rage was gripping her. Once again the innocent were being terrorised by the wrongdoers, and when the police came bursting in a little later she told them, 'I saw one of them with his face uncovered.'

'Would you recognise him again?' she was asked. 'You appear to be the only member of the public who was around at the time.'

'Yes. I would know him,' she said steadily, as the implications of what she was saying began to grip her. She was the only one the constable had said. It was history repeating itself. Her dad had been a witness and he'd ended up having to move to another part of the country.

The officer was asking for her name and address and even with dismay spiralling inside her she didn't hesitate.

'We'll be in touch,' he said, and went to see if anyone else had any information, but as the staff had been forced to lie face down and the robbers had covered their heads it wasn't likely.

As Helena wrapped Blake's present her hands were trembling. Until her father had told her about him being under witness protection because he'd given evidence, she'd never had any contact with the law or the lawless, but now it seemed as if they were everywhere she turned.

It didn't help, being in love with a police surgeon. She was on the fringe of it because of that. She still felt that there was more to it than Blake had told her regarding the woman who'd fallen from the balcony, but she supposed if he'd wanted her to know he would have told her, and he *was* committed to keeping his dealings with the police under wraps.

And then this afternoon the last thing she had expected to happen had brought her into the web of crime again. What would Blake say when she told him that she'd been pushed into the same sort of situation as her dad had found himself in?

As she gazed unseeingly into space she couldn't possibly visualise how he would react. He might think it all a big bind, having rescued her from one set of dangerous circumstances only for her to be involved in another. The word 'nuisance' sprang to mind.

He would be horrified when he knew that it had been when she had been buying him a gift that she'd become involved. It wouldn't go down well at all, especially with his continual insistence that he didn't want any thanks. But the photograph and frame weren't a thank-you present. They were a birthday gift.

She decided that Blake wasn't going to know about the afternoon's happenings until after they'd had the birthday meal. The last thing she wanted was to spoil his evening with Rowena.

When he picked her up he said immediately, 'What's wrong? You look pale and peaky.'

She managed a smile. Having dressed with special care in one of her favourite evening outfits and applied a liberal mount of make-up to conceal her pallor, she'd hoped to get away without Blake noticing that she wasn't exactly sparkling, but typically he'd picked up on her drained expression right away.

'I'm fine,' she fibbed. 'Just a bit tired, that's all.'

She'd decided to keep her birthday greetings until they got to Rowena's. That way, if their hostess was intending it to be a surprise birthday meal, she wouldn't be letting the cat out of the bag in advance.

Tonight Blake looked more gorgeous than ever. He was in casual clothes, a black cashmere sweater and grey trousers that achieved a lithe sort of elegance that would have had her heart beating faster if she hadn't been so worked up about the robbery.

Rowena was radiant in a long blue evening dress that made the silver of her hair glisten in the light of the lamps. They were all dressed to kill, Helena thought wryly, and would do justice to the beautifully set table and the food being placed upon it, but as far as she was concerned the evening had been spoilt. She'd been touched again by something unpleasant and couldn't get it out of her mind.

At the end of the meal Rowena picked up a package lying on a nearby chest of drawers and passed it over to Blake.

'Happy birthday, my dear,' she said.

'Oh! Thank you,' he said. 'I'd almost forgotten what day it was.

'What's this, Rowena?' he exclaimed, as he eyed its contents.

'It's papers for you to sign, Blake,' she said softly. 'I'm giving you the house and the land. I've decided to go into a very nice nursing home not too far away and nothing would make me happier than to know that one day your children will play in the gardens and sleep in the bedrooms. A family is what this place has been short of for many years. It's up to you to do something about it.'

Helena's mind was whirling, her face warm with embarrassment at being present on such an occasion. Was Rowena presuming too much, or did their hostess know something she didn't?

'I can't let you do this, Rowena,' he said incredulously.

'Too late,' she said calmly. 'I've done it, and, please, don't end up living here alone as I've done.'

And what was that supposed to mean? Blake wondered. Was he being given a nudge in the right direction? Rowena knew he was in love with Helena and what had just happened made it clear that she approved of his choice, but what of the young nurse who was sitting transfixed beside him?

Was she going to want to live here with him and fill the house with the children that Rowena longed to see? Helena had told him she was in love with him but they'd never got around to discussing the implications of it.

Had she been having thoughts of them living together? A partnership instead of a commitment, which would leave them free to break away if they wanted to? He'd been so busy keeping her at a distance he hadn't a clue about her thoughts on marriage. But he knew what his were.

'I have something for you, too,' Helena said, breaking into his thoughts, and she placed a flat parcel in his hand.

'So you knew it was my birthday, then,' he said with a smile.

She nodded. 'Rowena told me.'

'That's lovely, Helena!' he exclaimed, when he saw her face smiling up at him out of the ill fated frame.

'I'm glad you like it,' she said weakly, and thought that it was as well that he liked something she'd done today, because he wasn't going to be too pleased about the rest when she told him. She would be bringing back all his anxieties and yet what else could she have done other than agree to help the police? If her dad could do it, so could she...

*   *   *

'Will you come in for a moment?' she asked flatly when they got back to the cottage later.

'Only on one condition,' he said smilingly. 'That you tell me what's wrong. Something's been bugging you all evening and if it's to do with what Rowena said about me filling her house with children, don't feel that I'm going to take her up on it and have you for evermore with a child at your breast. Just a couple will do.'

He was happier than she'd ever seen him. Talking as if he wanted to marry her. That he felt the same as she did. She wished she didn't have to tell him about the robbery. It would ruin his evening, but as long as Blake saw it from the same angle as herself they would cope.

He didn't. He was aghast.

'You were caught up in the middle of a robbery?' he cried. 'And came face to face with one of them?' He was pacing up and down her small sitting room like a caged beast. '*And* you've told the police you would know him again. You realise what this means, Helena. You could be in the same position as your father if they get them. Stressed out, on the move all the time, forever looking over your shoulder.'

'Yes, I know,' she admitted stubbornly, 'but they terrorised the manager and everyone else who was in the shop. I owe it to them to speak up.'

'And supposing they were a gang similar to the Kelsalls. What then?'

'*They* operate miles away from here, in the town where we used to live,' she protested.

'I know that,' he said grimly. 'I'm not suggesting it *was* them. I said *like* them. And they *are* known in these parts. Kenny Kelsall was nearly imprisoned here. I suspect he would have been if your father hadn't been moved to this area.'

'How do you know?'

'It came up in conversation when I was at the prison the other day.'

Helena felt her face stretch. 'And you never thought to tell me!'

His jawline was tight, eyes cool. 'Why should I want to alarm you? And in any case it's water under the bridge. But you remember the body I was asked to examine at the hotel?'

'Yes.'

'The woman was the only witness in a big criminal case, and you saw what happened to her. She was got at within hours. So, you see, I'm not going to allow you to get involved in this robbery case. If they ask you to testify or identify this fellow, you must refuse.'

Helena was observing him in angry amazement.

'That is the last thing I expected you to say. *I* will decide if I'm going to get involved,' she said coldly, 'and if you're so concerned about my safety, why didn't you tell me what you'd heard about Kelsall and that the woman at the hotel was going to be a prosecution witness?

'I'm not a child, Blake. I might have behaved a bit like one in those first days after I lost my dad, but I have to fight my own battles and I think it's insulting that you weren't straight with me. I knew that night when you'd been called out to the hotel that there was something wrong, but you kept fobbing me off with excuses instead of telling me the truth.'

'Have you quite finished?' he asked in a voice that was dangerously calm. 'Maybe you see now why I haven't been falling at your feet. I've had too much on my mind concerning other aspects of your life. But my halo's slipping now, is it? Shall I take off my socks so that you can see my feet of clay? I'm sorry that I disappoint you. But if caring and protecting you is a crime, I'm guilty. I'll talk to you again, Helena, when you're in a more reasonable mood.'

'That's not likely to happen,' she snapped, and with an angry lift of one eyebrow he went, leaving her to think disconsolately that he'd forgotten to tell her to lock up. Not that she needed reminding. After what she'd just heard, there was no possibility that she would forget.

As the minutes ticked by her bravado oozed away. Choking back tears, Helena thought that if this was how it was going to be all the time, she would be better off going back to Australia. She would at least have peace of mind out there. But there would be no Blake.

Maybe there was already no Blake. She'd never seen him angry before and he'd certainly been that. He'd gone stomping off and she would be lucky if he had anything to say to her the next time they met.

She'd been right when she'd thought it would spoil his evening but hadn't expected it to be to such a degree. When she closed her eyes she could see Rowena's smile when she'd told him that the house was going to be his. There was a deep affection there and she felt it would have been extended to herself in a less complicated situation.

Her heart twisted at the memory of how he'd spoken as if *they* might live there one day...with their children. There was nothing she would love more than to be able to give him a family to make up for the one he'd lost.

But they were always bogged down by the misdeeds of others. She'd walked into a robbery that afternoon and become enmeshed in the aftermath of it, and after what had happened previously she couldn't blame Blake for being angry.

She wasn't going to make any moves towards contacting the police, she decided. It would be up to them to get in touch with her, and if and when they did she would make her decision then. No one could force her to testify. Just as no one could make her not testify.

In the midst of her troubled reasoning her main concern was the damage that it had caused to their relationship. Blake had belittled her love for him by saying that he'd had more important things to think about, and she'd mocked his concern for her. What a mess!

Maybe on Monday, back at the practice, they could patch things up, but she wasn't hopeful. They'd damaged the idyll, the precious thing they'd created, and she prayed that what they'd done would be repairable.

On Sunday Helena got up full of good intentions. Monday was too far off. She had to speak to him now. Make things right between them. If she loved Blake she should be prepared to consider his wishes, she told herself, even though he'd taken a stance that she hadn't expected.

Her determination lasted until she went into the hall and saw an envelope on the mat. Her name was on the front in a familiar bold scrawl and as she read its contents she groaned.

'I'm at a medical conference in Bristol for three days from tomorrow and have decided to drive down today. We both need a cooling-off period. But I do repeat, don't get involved, Helena. No one can make you.'

He'd just signed it 'Blake' and her comment about mending bridges came back to mind. Bridges didn't come any bigger or more broken than this one.

As Blake had driven home the night before he'd been seething. He'd been basking in his success at keeping Helena safe and secure, and as if an imp of mischief had been following them around she'd walked into an armed robbery.

He'd been on top of the world until she'd told him that and for once his habitual calm had deserted him. He admired her desire to do the honourable thing, but it could be very risky, as he'd told her in no uncertain terms. Surely she understood that he couldn't bear it if anything happened to her too. He was strong in every part of his life but that. Didn't she see that he could only endure so much? But it had ended up with Mr Perfect not being so perfect after all.

His smile was wry. He'd fallen off his pedestal all right. He supposed that as he worked with the police he should be on their side, but this time he wasn't. He was on his side...and hers.

He was in love with the green-eyed stranger from the far north and instead of telling her so he'd just alienated himself from her.

The conference wasn't an excuse. He'd intended telling her last night that he would be away for a few days, but all thought of that had been banished by what she'd had to tell him. Maybe by the time he got back she would have seen reason, and if she hadn't, what then?

It wasn't the same without him, Helena thought as Monday dragged by. Jane was back and they were busy enough, but it still felt as if every moment was an hour and she thought dismally that this was what life would be like without him.

The other two partners were coping with Blake's patients and Maxine wasn't feeling too chirpy either. She'd heard from somewhere that he was going to get Rowena's house and fancied herself playing the hostess there. But if the way he looked at the young nurse who'd come muscling into the practice was anything to go by, he had other plans.

She wasn't exactly antagonistic towards Helena, but Maxine always made sure she knew that her face didn't fit as far as she was concerned, and now she was making a point of Helena being within earshot when she announced to Darren, 'Blake and I spoke on the phone before he left. I'm having him over at my place for a meal when he gets home on Wednesday.'

'Get that,' Jane said in a low voice. 'Methinks it was for your benefit.'

'Probably,' Helena remarked flatly.

It would just make it longer before she saw him again, but see him she must, at the first opportunity, even though she didn't know what she was going to say when she did.

'So how is everything at the practice?' he asked Maxine on the Wednesday night as they ate the meal she'd prepared.

Dining with her was the last thing he'd wanted to do, but she'd been so insistent when he'd spoken to her before leaving for Bristol it had been difficult to refuse. Yet it hadn't stopped him from thinking that here was a woman anxious for his company, and the one he was longing to see hadn't been in touch. But he was going to put things right the moment he saw her. He was going to ask Helena to marry him. She'd told him how *she* felt. Now it was up to him.

'Fine,' Maxine said in answer to his question, adding after a moment's hesitation, 'Though we've been short on practice nurses.'

He nodded.

'Jane still off with that husband of hers, then?'

'No, Jane is back,' she said casually. 'It's the new one. The Harris girl. She's in hospital.'

He almost dropped his knife and fork. 'Why? What's happened to her?'

'Run-of-the-mill sort of thing,' she said, still adopting a casual tone.

'What, for heaven's sake?' he bellowed.

'An ovarian cyst...that had ruptured.'

'Ruptured! Helena must have been in some pain, then. When did this occur?'

'Yesterday. She was operated on last night.'

'And you never mentioned it when I rang this morning to confirm what time I'd be back?'

'What would have been the point? You were miles away. You couldn't have done anything.'

'I could have gone straight to the hospital instead of coming here, which I imagine was the very thing you wanted to prevent. Helena has no one, Maxine, and yet you begrudge her my time and care. Stay away from me in future!' Grabbing his belongings, he strode out of the room with a haste that left her in no doubt where his affections lay.

CHAPTER EIGHT

THE stomach pain had come out of the blue on Monday evening. It had been bearable at first but had steadily got worse, and by the middle of the night Helena had known she had to get help. But where from?

If Blake had been at home she wouldn't have needed to think twice, but he hadn't been and as she'd lain hunched up in agony she would have given everything she'd possessed to have him with her.

She'd felt she couldn't ask Jane to come round in the middle of the night, which left only the emergency doctor services or a direct call for an ambulance. She'd never felt so alone in her life. Something had been wrong in her stomach area and she'd been apprehensive about what it might be.

It had been the wrong place for her appendix and she hadn't vomited or shown any other signs of a gastric upset, so it had to be something else. She'd prayed it hadn't been anything to do with her womb or ovaries, but as the pain had become past bearing she'd put those worries to one side and phoned for an ambulance.

When it had come, one of the paramedics had examined her. 'You're not pregnant, are you, Helena? It could be a miscarriage,' she'd said.

Helena shook her head. 'No. Definitely not.'

'OK. Let's get you to someone who can sort you out. Is there anyone who can come with you?'

'No,' she told her weakly, 'But I'm not bothered about that. Just get me some help.'

She *was* bothered, bothered a lot. She wanted Blake. If she was going to die she wanted him beside her. But she couldn't let that happen, could she? It was the thing that haunted him, history repeating itself.

After being given some pain relief, she was able to concentrate on what the doctor in A and E was saying when he came to tell her what they'd found after scanning.

'You have an ovarian cyst that has ruptured,' he told her. 'That's where all the pain has been coming from. Under normal circumstances they're usually painless, but not in this sort of situation.'

She observed him with anxious eyes. 'You won't have to remove the ovary, will you?'

'Can't promise,' he'd said. 'Depends on what we find when we open you up, but we'll do our best to save it.'

She turned her head into the pillow and prayed that nothing was going to occur that would prevent her from having children.

Her first words on coming round from the anaesthetic were, 'Have I still got two ovaries?'

'Yes, you have at the moment,' she'd been told, 'but we have to do tests on the cyst to see if it was cancerous.'

Helena nodded. She knew the score. Most ovarian cysts were benign, but there was always the chance that one wasn't and until they knew for certain the gnawing anxiety wasn't going to go away.

She phoned the practice before going down to Theatre on Tuesday to let them know where she was, and when one of the receptionists answered she'd asked her to inform Jane and the other two partners.

Jane visited her on Tuesday evening and was appalled that she'd had to go through the ordeal alone.

'Dr Pemberton will be most upset when he knows what's happened,' she said. 'Maxine intends getting her claws into him the moment he gets back and she won't be rushing to tell him that you've had to be operated on. Do you remember how she made sure we all know he's going to her place for a meal when he arrives home tomorrow night? It will suit her fine that you're not around.'

'Surely she wouldn't wish this on me!' Helena exclaimed.

'Of course she would,' Jane said laughingly. 'She'll be disappointed that it's not terminal.'

'It might be,' Helena told her, joining in the laughter in spite of her anxieties.

'I'm sorry,' Jane had said contritely. 'One shouldn't joke about such matters. How long before you know whether it was malignant?'

'I'm not sure. They've told me I'll be in here until the end of the week so I'm hoping the results will have come through by then,' Helena told her. Her voice thickened. 'Do you think Blake will still love me if I have no ovaries?'

'Steady on,' her friend protested. 'We're talking about *one* ovary that *might* be suspect. Not two that have to be removed. Of course it won't make any difference to him. He won't see you as a breeding machine no matter how much he wants children with you.'

'Yes, but I wouldn't be a whole woman, would I?'

'*You'd* be a whole woman no matter what you had missing,' Jane said gently. 'Now, get some sleep or they'll be telling me off for tiring you.'

Beverley, the practice manager, called in first thing Wednesday morning and one of the receptionists popped in during her lunch-hour. It was nice to see them, and even Darren, carrying gaudy blooms, in the late afternoon was a welcome sight, but she wanted Blake. Her world wasn't going to right itself until he appeared.

As Blake drove to the hospital his mind was in chaos. His first thought when he'd heard where Helena was had been that she'd been attacked. And yet within seconds, before Maxine had even begun to explain, he'd known it wasn't likely, not unless the police had caught the villains who'd robbed the jeweller's and she'd agreed to testify. But the processes of the law didn't move that fast, neither did the catching of criminals.

When had she started to be ill? he wondered. He hoped it hadn't been in the middle of the night when she'd been alone. And how serious had the operation been? Serious enough, he'd like to bet, if the cyst had ruptured.

But he wasn't going to think any further than that until he'd seen her and spoken to the doctor who'd operated. Why they hadn't rung him from the practice to tell him what was going on he didn't know.

He'd spoken to Maxine each day about practice matters while he'd been away and she'd never said anything which, he supposed, wasn't surprising as she'd never had a good word for Helena since the day she'd joined them.

Well, Maxine had well and truly put her foot in it. She'd let him sit opposite her and eat a leisurely meal when all the time she'd known that Helena was in hospital.

She was dozing when he appeared at the side of her bed, but the moment his shadow fell across her she opened her eyes.

'I thought you were dining with Maxine,' she said drowsily, as he took her hand in his.

'I was,' he said gently, 'until she told me where you were, and after that I couldn't eat another mouthful. I was out of her place like an arrow from a bow. But I'm not here to talk about her. How are you feeling?'

'Sore and apprehensive.'

He didn't question that comment, just nodded. 'How serious was the op?' he asked.

'I'm still intact,' she told him, averting her eyes, 'but that may be only temporary if they find the cyst was malignant.'

'So it's wait-and-see time,' he said gravely. 'You do realise that, whatever the verdict, it won't make any difference to us.'

'It will to me,' she said flatly. 'You want children and if I can't give them to you we might as well finish it now.'

'That's crazy talk, Helena,' he protested.

'Is it? You once said that you were having to be sensible for both of us. Well, now it's my turn to be the sensible one.'

'We haven't been together five minutes and we're disagreeing,' he said exasperatedly. 'Your wellbeing is all that matters to me, but I won't press the point. Let's just wait and see, and in the meantime tell me how all this came about.'

'The pain came on early Monday evening,' she told him, 'and as the night progressed it became so bad I had to send for an ambulance.'

His face was grim.

'So you were alone?'

'Well, yes. I haven't found myself a new man while you've been away.'

'I'm glad you can see the funny side of it,' he said heavily. 'I would have been frantic if I'd known you were in that state with no one to look after you.'

'I'm sorry, Blake,' she said contritely. 'Believe me, it wasn't funny at the time. I would have given anything to have had you there.'

'I can think of one way of making sure we're never out of touch again and being able to keep an eye on you on a permanent basis,' he said softly. 'Will you marry me, Helena?'

Her eyes filled with tears. It was what she'd longed to hear him say but now it wasn't so simple. There were other things to consider. In the last few days her life had been turned upside down once more and until she'd got the test results she couldn't think straight.

'Let's wait until the results on the cyst come through.'

He sighed. 'That's one of the reasons I'm asking you now. So that you understand that I want you no matter what. If I'd waited until afterwards you might think I wasn't taking any chances when the truth of the matter is that I just simply want you to be my wife.'

She shook her head stubbornly. 'You are the most wonderful man I've ever met,' she told him chokingly, 'but if there's a chance that I might have cancer or maybe won't be able to give you children, I can't marry you. I don't want you having to make sacrifices on my behalf. You deserve better.'

'I think you should let me be the judge of that,' he said tightly.

Helena took his face between her hands and observed him tenderly. 'Not this time. This is my decision, Blake, and in the meantime, while we're waiting for the results, give some thought to the reasons you gave for marrying me. You said it was because you wanted to always be there for me in a crisis and have me permanently under your wing. But shouldn't it be because you simply can't exist without me? Rather than a desire to be my full-time protector?'

He got to his feet. 'I always thought if I ever proposed to another woman it would be a joyous occasion,' he said levelly, 'not a soulless discussion about the whys and wherefores of the arrangement.

'The nurses have told me not to tire you, so maybe this isn't the time to hold an investigation on our innermost feelings. I'm going home to unpack, Helena. I'll be in to see you some time tomorrow.' His voice softened. 'None of this really matters, does it? Everything pales into insignificance when compared to you making a full recovery.' And with a fleeting kiss on her hot cheek he began to walk away, a tall, lithe figure moving towards the outside world she'd so suddenly been shut away from.

When he got into his car Blake didn't start it immediately. He felt like a pricked balloon. Helena had made his proposal sound like a business arrangement. Of course he couldn't exist without her and if he hadn't made that clear it was because their lives were always enmeshed in anxieties.

Hopefully her sudden illness would turn out to be an unpleasant scare soon forgotten, but alternatively it might turn out to be not so simple and have far-reaching consequences on their lives. It had come out of the blue and she was dealing with it bravely, putting his needs before her own.

But he didn't want that. He wanted them to be at peace with each other. The disagreement about her giving evidence on the robbery was still hanging over them.

When he called in at the hospital the next day the matters discussed previously weren't mentioned. Helena had been told that the results of the tests on the cyst would be available that afternoon, and Blake told her that he would call back later.

And so for the short time that he was there they talked about everything except the rift between them. The practice, Rowena, who was going ahead with her preparations regarding the nursing home, and what Helena was going to do when she was discharged.

'I think you should come to my place until you're feeling well enough to come back to the practice,' he suggested, carefully refraining from any comments regarding further surgery.

'I feel well enough to cope,' she said. 'I'll be fine at the cottage.'

So we're still wallowing in the pit of mis-understanding, he thought frustratedly. Where on earth do we go from here? But he concealed his dismay and said calmly, 'Sure. You know best how you feel.'

When he called back that afternoon she'd gone, and as he stood transfixed by the empty bed a passing nurse said, 'Helena Harris was discharged early this afternoon. She made good progress and has been told to come back to see the doctor next week.'

'And the results of the cancer tests?'

She smiled.

'You know I can't divulge that, Dr Pemberton. She'll have to tell you herself.'

There was dread inside him mixed with hurt. All Helena had needed to do was pick up a phone to let him know she was going home and he would have come to fetch her. Were the results so bad that she couldn't bear to tell him?

When she opened the door to his knock he saw that she was very pale and the anxiety in him increased.

'So what was the verdict?' he asked, without wasting any time on small talk.

She managed a watery smile. 'I'm clear. It wasn't cancerous.'

Blake felt his nerve ends tighten.

'Well, thanks for letting me know *and* leaving the hospital without a word. I've been going crazy with worry on your behalf and this is how you treat me. You can forget the marriage proposal. I would have loved and cherished you, no matter what, but your insensitivity and selfishness are something I *won't* be able to stomach.

'You are all talk and no integrity, Helena. You say that you love me, but when I ask you to marry me you use the threat of cancer as an excuse to keep me at arm's length, and just to be on the safe side, if that didn't materialise you start questioning my motives as a reason to keep me dangling. I hope you can understand yourself, because I'm damned if I can.'

And with hurt and anger still inside him he went.

But before he'd got to the end of the road shame was wiping out any other emotion. He'd been so busy letting off steam he'd never told Helena what wonderful news it was to hear that she was clear of cancer. Only the day before he'd been holding forth that a good result on her health problems was all that mattered and now, when she'd got that, he'd been ranting on about his own annoyances.

But did he want this kind of thing in his life? Never knowing where he was with Helena? The answer was yes. *She* wasn't to blame for all the unpleasant things that had happened to her in recent months. *She'd* been the impulsive one, telling him she loved him, but *she* was the one who, though she hadn't realised it, needed time, and if that was all it would take to get them back on line he would see that she had it.

After Blake had gone Helena stood staring at the closed door, willing him to come back through it, but he didn't and she supposed she couldn't blame him.

When they'd told her at the hospital that she could go she'd just slung the few belongings she'd taken with her into a bag, had rung for a taxi and departed, light-headed with relief and desperate to be by herself.

She'd wanted Blake to be there when she got the results and yet when it had come to the crunch she'd changed her mind. She was fed up with continually being a liability, she thought dismally, and Blake was a collector of lost sheep. He was even willing to marry her to keep her safely in the pen.

But she didn't want that. She wanted them to be even. Not with her as the shifting sand and him as the rock. That was why she'd fallen out with him over the robbery.

If only she could turn the clock back to when they'd first met, she thought wistfully. It had all been so simple then. She'd been the victim and he her saviour. At that time she'd been falling over herself to accept his help but now, because of her stupid pride, she was spurning it.

Blake had said she was insensitive and self-ish. Two words that could never be applied to him.

It was her first day back at the practice and he wasn't there. Helena was sick with disappointment. He'd phoned every day since she'd been discharged from the hospital and that had been it. Just a brief enquiry to make sure she was all right and then goodbye. When she'd tried to prolong the conversations the words had stuck in her throat. She had been pinning all her hopes on being back in his company at the practice and had now discovered he wasn't there.

'It's only a minor absence,' Jane assured her on seeing her downcast face. 'He's taking Rowena Maddox to the rest home. She's moving in today and won't Blake be the lucky one, being able to move into that gorgeous house of hers?'

'Yes, indeed,' Helena agreed weakly.

She'd blown her chances of sharing it with him. Though the house wasn't that important. She would live in a shack with him if they could develop a better understanding of what made each of them tick.

In her lunch-hour she went to get a card for Rowena to wish her happiness in her new surroundings, and as she was coming out of the shop Blake was there, buying a newspaper and looking tired and out of sorts.

'So you're back,' he said flatly, as if she'd brought the plague with her. 'Are you sure you're well enough to be on your feet all day?'

'Yes,' she said simply, resisting the urge to reach out and hold him close.

'I've been settling Rowena in,' he said as they walked back to the practice. 'I was intending taking the day off but it all went so smoothly she was bidding me be gone by late morning.'

She had to ask. 'So when are you moving?'

'Into her place, you mean?'

'Yes.'

'It depends.'

'On what?'

Helena was holding her breath. Was this the moment when they were going to put things right, or was she presuming too much?

She was.

'It depends on how long it takes for one or two alterations that I'm planning,' he said, as if they were merely acquaintances.

'Yes, those sorts of things do take time, don't they? It's a beautiful house. I'm sure you must have lots of plans for it,' she commented, as if only mildly interested, when all the time she was aching to hear all about what was going on.

'Oh, I have plans all right,' he said with an enthusiasm she felt was a bit overdone. 'You must come and have a look when it's all finished.'

'Sure,' she told him, still with the casual approach. 'Why don't you have a housewarming? I never got around to it, did I?'

They had reached the entrance to the surgery and he didn't take her up on the comment, just went striding off into his own room and that was that.

Helena was due to help Maxine with the antenatal clinic that afternoon, and as she made the preparations for examining the mothers-to-be the doctor was nowhere to be seen. The clock was ticking on and as there was still no sign of her Helena went to seek her out. She'd been there that morning, which had been essential with Blake being absent, but now appeared to have gone off on some pursuit of her own.

As Helena was querying her absence in Reception, Blake came out of his room and said, 'I've just found a note on my desk. Maxine is taking the afternoon off. She will be leaving us shortly and has gone to get acquainted with the partners in the practice that she's moving to.' He turned to Helena. 'So I'll take the antenatal clinic today.'

There was surprise on the faces of the staff, not least on Helena's. What had brought that about? she wondered. Maxine moving to pastures new. And fancy going off for the afternoon with just a note to say she'd gone.

Supposing Blake hadn't been back in time, and Darren was having to do her house calls as well as his own. It was the last thing *she'd* been expecting, having to work with Blake, and she didn't know whether to be glad or sorry.

As the afternoon progressed with the expectant mothers, all in different stages of pregnancy, taking their turns to be seen by him, Helena's mind kept going back to those moments when she'd told him she wouldn't marry him if she couldn't give him children. Was he remembering it, too, she wondered, and facing up to the fact that her fears had been banished and yet it wasn't getting them anywhere?

Gaynor Saxby was the oldest of the women present. In her late forties, she was delighted to be pregnant again now that her other children had flown the nest. However, her husband, who was with her, looked much less pleased than his wife.

'She's over the moon, my missus,' he told Helena while Blake was examining Gaynor, 'but I have my reservations about starting a family again at our time of life. It's risky, not just for her but for the baby. Suppose it turns out to have Down's syndrome? We could be dead by the time it reached its teens and then who would care for it?'

'You can ask for amniocentesis,' she told him. 'A small amount of the amniotic fluid that surrounds the baby is withdrawn and tested for any abnormalities.'

'Yes, I know,' he said, 'but we've been told there's a chance it might harm the child and Gaynor won't risk that.'

'Your wife is doing fine,' Blake told him as he came out of the cubicle. 'She's positively blooming.'

'Maybe,' the disgruntled husband said, 'but she won't be blooming when she's up half the night with it.'

'Maybe you should have used some kind of contraception, then,' Blake commented.

'We didn't think we needed to at our age.'

'If a woman is still ovulating, precautions are necessary if the couple want to avoid a pregnancy,' he reminded him, and swished back the curtains of the next cubicle which held the youngest of the expectant mothers, a sixteen-year-old schoolgirl.

'That went very well,' he said, when the last of them had departed. 'Not a single high blood pressure, haemorrhoids or signs of a breech birth. Next week they'll have the lot, you'll see.'

Helena was sterilising the instruments they'd been using and disposing of paper sheets and swabs. Intent on what she was doing, she wasn't aware that his glance was on the smooth skin at the back of her neck above the collar of her uniform.

He ached to touch her, to feel the sweet magic that was there every time they came into contact, but as his arms reached out for her she swung round and he let them fall slackly to his side.

'What?' she said.

'Nothing,' he replied flatly.

'You're still angry with me, aren't you?'

'Disenchanted might be a better word,' he said in the same tone. 'I thought we had a lot in common, but it seems I was mistaken. You made a mockery of my marriage proposal, after having been so eager for me to return your feelings, and then in spite of knowing how anxious I was regarding the test results you just floated off home without letting me know. So how do you expect me to be feeling, Helena? Over the moon?'

'I know it was wrong of me,' she said defiantly, 'but, Blake, nothing ever seems to go right for me. I seem to move from one trauma to another and I don't want it to be like that, with you always in charge and me like a millstone around your neck.'

He frowned. 'I don't understand where all this is coming from. It started with you insisting that you would help the police over the robbery at the jeweller's if they asked you to, and me insisting that you don't—a reasonable request, I would have thought, after all that's happened in the past. I could understand the ethics of it, but not the risk you were willing to take and from that time we've been totally out of tune.

'When you've decided what you want for us, you know where to find me. I get the impression, especially after the way you left the hospital without a word, that you're feeling you need some space, so take all the time you want.'

His glance was on the clock. 'It's time for afternoon surgery, and if Maxine isn't back and Darren is still on his rounds I'm going to be kept fully occupied. I suggest that *you* go home. You've been on your feet long enough for your first day back. Jane will cope without you for once.'

As she opened her mouth to protest he said, 'Don't argue, Helena. Do as I say.' And because she knew that he was right, she went.

What was the matter with her? Helena wondered as the autumn night wrapped itself around the cottage. Was she suffering from post-operative stress, or was she just being difficult? That was more likely. She'd been in the doldrums ever since they'd fallen out about the robbery. It had been their first disagreement and Blake was right. It had been the beginning of the distance between them.

She loved him, yet knew he must be hard put to believe it from the way she was behaving. She *was* tired, but her thoughts were too chaotic to expect sleep to come if she had an early night.

With sudden determination she decided that there was only one thing she wanted, his arms around her. On that thought she went out into the night and pointed the car towards the place where they'd first met, the cul-de-sac where her father had been in hiding.

Blake's house was in darkness and she groaned in frustration when there was no answer to her ring. Maybe the police had called him out, she thought. Or he'd had to go to the prison. Both thoughts were depressing. And if that wasn't the case, where else could he be?

Her face brightened. The house, of course. Rowena's gift to him. It made sense that was where he would be on the first night of his ownership. As far as she knew, the pleasant Mrs Porteous was staying on as his housekeeper and they would have things to discuss.

Would she be intruding if she turned up out of the blue? Possibly, but she didn't care. If they only ended up talking about the weather, she had to see him.

As she turned into the quiet lane where the house was situated she saw his car on the drive and her spirits lifted. It seemed as if he was already making his mark, sorting out the things he wanted to keep from those he didn't, as smoke was coming from the back of the house and there was a pungent smell of burning.

But when she went round to where the smoke was coming from Helena saw that it wasn't rubbish that was burning. It was something more valuable. The house. Her blood froze.

Flames were leaping up behind windows on the first floor and the smoke was billowing out of a nearby door, which was wide open. Was Blake inside? she thought frantically. And where was Mrs Porteous?

When she looked up she saw him at one of the windows, silhouetted against the flames with the limp figure of the housekeeper in his arms.

As she watched in horror Helena fumbled for her mobile, nerveless fingers dialling the emergency code. Then she was running towards the open door and the inferno.

When she stepped into a small back hallway Blake was coming down the stairs with his unconscious burden and she ran to help him.

'I've phoned the emergency services,' she gasped.

Red-rimmed eyes met hers in a blackened face and he nodded, indicating for her to go in front of him, back into the cool night air.

He laid the housekeeper on the grass and said hoarsely, 'See if you can bring her round, Helena, while I go back in for her dog. The poor little thing is terrified and she wouldn't move without it until the smoke got to her and she collapsed.'

'Don't go back inside,' she pleaded. 'If anything happens to you, I won't be able to bear it.'

Blake gave her a long, level look and without speaking he turned and went running back into the house. In that moment she understood how he must feel when *she* was in danger and it was a chastening feeling. But she had work to do. Bending over the unconscious woman, she began to try to resuscitate her.

As the housekeeper began to breathe again, making hoarse rasping sounds as she did so, the glass shattered in the windows above and Helena could hear the sound of woodwork and masonry falling.

She got to her feet. Blake was in there, risking his life for a poor frightened animal. She had to go to him. As she ran towards the open door once more, sirens wailing in the quiet night indicated that the fire services had arrived and, on observing what she had in mind, one of the firecrew jumped off the engine and grabbed her arm.

'Is someone in there?' he asked, as the rest of them sprang into action.

'Yes. He brought the old lady out and then went back in for her dog.'

'See to her, then, and leave the rest to us,' he said, and numbly she obeyed.

CHAPTER NINE

ONE of the firemen had dropped to his knees beside her with oxygen apparatus. 'I'm the trauma technician with the team,' he said as he put the mask over the housekeeper's face. 'Similar status to a paramedic. I can see that you know what you're doing.'

'I'm a nurse, and the man in there is a doctor,' she told him, eyeing the burning building in mute anguish. 'He's already been in there once. I'm terrified of what might be happening to him.'

'There he is!' the man cried, and she saw that Blake was being helped through the door, supported on each side by a member of the firecrew. Behind them was another firefighter, carrying the limp figure of the dog.

Leaving Mrs Porteous in the care of the trauma technician, Helena ran towards them, dreading what condition Blake would be in but humbly grateful that he was alive.

'The dog!' he croaked, gasping for air. 'See to the dog, Helena. That poor woman won't survive if anything's happened to her pet. How is she?'

'She's being given oxygen,' she told him, 'and the men will see to the dog. It's you I'm concerned about.'

There were burns on his forearm where'd he'd tried to protect his face. The thick dark pelt of his hair was singed, his eyebrows had almost disappeared and his clothes were scorched beyond recognition.

'I'm all right,' he wheezed, and immediately contradicted himself as his knees sagged and he fell at her feet.

They had all benefited from the oxygen, Blake, Mrs Porteous and the dog. And now he, Mrs Porteous and Helena were in the ambulance, with Helena hovering anxiously. The dog had been taken to the animal hospital.

'I told you to go home and rest,' Blake said, with his eyes on her white face.

'It's a good job I didn't,' she said drily. 'At least I came in useful. But what about your beautiful house?'

'That's the least of my worries,' he said sombrely. 'It can be repaired.' He glanced across at the elderly housekeeper who was under the watchful eye of a paramedic. 'Apart from smoke inhalation, that poor woman is in a state of severe shock.'

'And you are unblemished, I suppose,' she said gently. 'Could you just for once spare a thought for yourself? You're all singed and sizzled. I thought I was going to lose you…and I do love you so.'

He managed a gargoyle sort of smile.

'Only the good die young, Helena.'

'Then you should have gone long ago.'

'Rubbish,' he croaked, and when she looked up the hospital gates were looming up in front of them.

The housekeeper had been checked over and then admitted to one of the wards. Her breathing problems were less acute than Blake's because she hadn't been in the smoke as long as he had, but there was her age to consider and, as he'd already pointed out, she was in a state of shock so the hospital would be keeping her under observation for the next few days.

Mrs Porteous had no idea how the fire had started but was experiencing great mortification that it should have occurred on the day that the house had become Blake's.

'The firecrew will be checking for possible causes,' Blake told her when she expressed her concern, 'and in the meantime, don't worry about a thing. Just concentrate on your recovery.'

'But where will I live?' she sobbed.

'It was only your part of the house that was on fire,' he told her gently. 'There are other rooms you can have.'

He'd insisted on seeing her before he was bedded down himself and as Helena had listened to him there were tears in her eyes as she remembered how she'd behaved when he'd asked her to marry him.

He *was* her rock and what was wrong with that? She was blessed to have a man like Blake Pemberton in her life. She couldn't blame him if he was thinking that *she* was the one with the feet of clay.

It seemed that he might be. As the porter was pushing him towards a small side ward, Blake said hoarsely, 'No one's asking you to change your priorities because of what's happened today, Helena. You're entitled to see things in a different light to what I do. I don't want you going all soft on me because I've had a bad day.'

Bad day! she wanted to shriek at him. You could have been killed! Didn't you hear me when I said how much I love you?

Instead, she said nothing. He was in no fit state to listen. His burns had been dressed, his lungs checked, and he still needed oxygen, though not as frequently.

What Blake needed now was to be away from her and all the problems she posed, and once he was settled she kissed him swiftly on the cheek and told him, 'It's my turn to do the hospital visiting this time. I'll be in to see you tomorrow.' And before he could comment she'd gone.

So much for tact and understanding, Blake thought as he eased himself back against the pillows. Helena had been frantic during the whole episode, but the last thing he wanted was for her to start feeling she had to be there for him.

He hadn't started the fire to bring her to heel, he thought wryly. In fact, he hadn't a clue what had caused it. Mrs Porteous had her own suite of rooms at the rear of the house and when he'd parked his car he'd looked up and been horrified to see flames glowing behind the windows of what was her sitting room.

Knowing that she had her own kitchen, he'd thought at first that it must be a chip-pan fire, that being the most common cause of fires in the kitchen, but when he'd flung himself up the stairs there had been nothing ablaze on the cooker.

The fire had started in the sitting room where she'd been watching television, and by the time he'd arrived it had been about to spread to the rest of the apartment.

She'd told him that she'd dozed off after such a busy day and had woken up to find the room full of smoke. She'd gone to grab the dog but the terrified animal hadn't allowed her near it and she'd refused to leave without it.

The house was insured. He wasn't worried about that. Though Rowena would have a shock when she heard what had happened. But, hopefully, now she was settled in her new home, it mightn't upset her too much.

He intended having a lot of work done on the place in any case, so the repairing of fire damage would be just one more job to do. He would be feeling more enthusiastic if he knew that Helena was going to be involved. That one day they would be living there together. But what he'd just said to her wasn't going to improve matters, was it?

Yet the fact remained. He *didn't* want her to feel bound to him because of the fire, though if it had created a situation where their roles had been reversed, maybe she would have a better understanding of his feelings.

The staff at the practice were dumbfounded the next morning when they heard about the fire. All except Maxine who smiled a little satisfied smile when she heard the news.

'You don't think she's into arson, do you?' Jane whispered. 'I wouldn't put it past her. You know, sour grapes and all that.'

Helena shook her head. 'No. Blake rang this morning to let me know that the fire service says it was faulty wiring. He doesn't think the house has been rewired since it was built. Rowena would be horrified if she knew that her generosity could have cost him and Mrs Porteous their lives. Renewing the wiring was on his list of jobs to be done but the fire occurred before he had the chance.'

He *had* rung that morning just as she'd been leaving the cottage. When she'd heard his croaky voice coming over the line her heart had leapt, but that had been all he'd wanted her for. However, before he'd rung off she'd reminded him that she would be calling at the hospital in her lunch hour.

'Don't bother,' he'd said. 'I'm being discharged. I'll be home by then.'

'So I'll call round at the house.'

'There's no need, Helena,' he'd said with a sigh, as if she'd been tiresome. 'I'll be back in harness tomorrow and will see you then.'

'I hope you're satisfied that the punishment fits the crime,' she'd flared angrily. 'Because you *are* punishing me, aren't you? Rubbing it in that I got it all wrong and now that I have the chance to show *you* some tender, loving care, you won't let me.'

If he'd had any reply to make to that he hadn't had the chance as she'd hung up.

Although her heart clenched at the sight of his burns and reddened skin when they came face to face the next day, she refrained from any further comment.

As winter's chill followed autumn and the surgery became busier with seasonal coughs and colds, Helena sometimes thought that she was living in a cold climate of her own and could see no signs of a thaw.

She and Blake were pleasantly polite to each other at the practice but it didn't go any further than that. If she ever found him on her doorstep she would collapse with the shock, she told herself.

All right, he was very busy with repairs and alterations at Rowena's old house, but not so busy that she didn't sometimes see him dining in the Swan or driving towards the town at weekends.

Maxine had left, with little regret on the part of the staff. A new partner was due to take her place any day. He was elderly and would make it an all-male partnership.

Helena didn't know what Blake thought about Maxine's departure and had no idea that it was connected with herself. That his rage on the night when she'd delayed telling him that his young protégée had been in hospital had finally made her realise that she was wasting her time hankering after him.

Darren had got engaged to a pleasant blonde and was already house-hunting, and as she looked around her Helena felt that everyone's life was moving on except hers.

There'd been no word from the police about the robbery at the jeweller's so it seemed as if they hadn't caught the thieves and she'd put that unpleasant incident to the back of her mind.

One night when she was feeling bored and lonely she rang one of the nurses she'd made friends with in Australia. Deborah had signed up for another year and she said, 'Why don't you come back, Helena? There are still vacancies out here for trained nurses.'

'I don't think so,' she said slowly. 'But I'll let you know if I change my mind.'

It was a thought, she supposed. With each day that passed she was becoming more convinced there was nothing for her here. Blake had obviously decided that he'd done his bit as far as she was concerned and didn't want any more complications. Short of going down on her knees, there wasn't a lot she could do about it.

Mrs Porteous was installed back at the house in a different set of rooms and the wiring had all been renewed. When she'd asked Blake about her he'd said that she appeared to have recovered from the trauma of the fire but that he felt she would feel better when he was in residence there himself.

'And when is that likely to be?' she'd asked, trying not to sound too interested.

'Soon, I hope,' he'd replied, and Helena had thought achingly that, hearing them, no one would have believed that there had once been a strong possibility of her living there with him. It was as if the present had blotted out the past.

In early December he announced that the house was finished and that on Saturday night all the staff of the practice were invited to a housewarming.

'You'll come, I hope,' he said when they were alone for a few seconds in the nurses' room.

'I'm not sure,' she said.

It would be like a turning of the knife, being shown around the house where she'd hoped to bring up their children. Who was being insensitive now?

'Please, do,' he persisted, and just as she was thinking that maybe Blake really did want her there, he blighted her hopes by saying, 'It will look odd if you're the only member of staff who doesn't turn up.'

'Oh, well, I'll have to come, then, won't I?' she said sarcastically. 'Never let it be said that I refused such a tempting invitation.'

'I wish I understood you better, Helena,' he told her flatly. 'I had plans for that house, big plans. I still have, but they've changed. I might turn it into a nursing home or a care centre for troubled adolescents.'

'I see,' she said slowly. 'So you're not going to live there yourself?'

'I haven't made up my mind,' he replied, and when one of the receptionists called across to say there was a medical rep to see him he went, leaving her more in the doldrums than ever.

On the evening of the housewarming Helena's spirits were at their lowest ebb. She felt as if she'd been invited on sufferance like Cinderella, but *she'd* been the lucky one, she'd ended up with the prince.

But, she thought defiantly, like Cinderella she was going to look her best, and reaching her favourite green silk dress from the wardrobe she began to get ready.

She'd had her hair cut that afternoon and now the shining russet swathe of it had been replaced by a short curly cut that accentuated her high cheekbones and made her eyes look big and luminous. Would Blake notice? she wondered as she stood in front of the mirror. Or would he be too busy disapproving of her?

As she was about to leave the phone rang. It was her friend Deborah from Australia, wanting to know if she'd changed her mind about going out there again.

'The hospital would love to have you back,' she said. 'When I told them you were considering it, they asked me to try to persuade you.'

'I can't talk now,' she told her. 'I'm just off to a party. I'll ring you when I get back.'

The house was finished and it looked good. All it lacked now was its mistress, Blake thought as he stood waiting to greet his guests. He wasn't going to turn it into a nursing home or a care home for teenagers with problems unless Helena made it clear that they had no future.

He couldn't believe the tame excuse he'd come up with when she'd hesitated about coming. Saying she would be the odd one out! Why hadn't he said straight out that the whole idea was a strategy to get her on the premises without giving her a chance to refuse?

Surely when she saw how beautiful he'd made it she would want to live there, but he didn't want the house pleading his cause. He wanted it to be that she would be willing to live with him anywhere just as long as they really loved each other. That was how *he* felt. Hopefully he might discover her feelings regarding it tonight.

It would be a lovely place to bring up children, but that wasn't the issue either. He'd waited a long time before finding someone he wanted to marry and if he couldn't have her he wanted no one else.

She was the last to arrive and when he opened the door to her his pulses leapt. The cropped hairstyle was enchanting. It enhanced the long smooth stem of her neck and the bare shoulders beneath it. The house would fit her like a glove, he thought. She would bring light and joy to it.

But there wasn't anything light and joyous about the cool hand stretched out to shake his.

'I hope I'm not late,' she said. 'I had a phone call from Australia just as I was leaving the cottage.'

'Australia,' he echoed, jolted out of his sweet imaginings.

'Yes.' He took her wrap. 'Are you going to give us all the guided tour?'

'Later,' he said, still trying to adjust to the comment about Australia. 'The others are all here. Let me get you a drink.'

'Sure,' she said, hoping she wasn't going to choke on her disappointment.

Blake had given her a long lingering look when he'd opened the door but he hadn't said anything complimentary. Maybe these days he was immune to her attractions. Though was he *likely* to be overcome by admiration after the way they'd been in recent weeks?

As he showed them around the house she was wishing that she hadn't come. Now that she'd actually seen the large airy rooms and beautiful furnishings, they would plague her memory.

But when they came to the wing that had been damaged by the fire there were different mind pictures to contend with. She could see the flames licking greedily at the windows and Blake holding the unconscious housekeeper in his arms.

Did anything matter as long as he was alive? she thought tremulously. It could all have gone so horribly wrong, but for once the fates had smiled on them.

The others had sauntered on ahead but Helena felt as if she was rooted to the spot. She shuddered. There were too many horrible things in their pasts, and as if he'd read her mind Blake said from nearby, 'As you once complained that I keep things from you, perhaps I'd better tell you that I've made some discreet enquiries and so far the police haven't got a result on the robbery at the jeweller's. They've got one or two leads they're following up but no joy yet.'

'I see,' she said quietly. 'So for the time being I have a reprieve.'

'Yes,' he agreed. 'We both have. But I still think it's lunacy if you get involved.'

'I still can't believe you're saying that!' she protested. 'You of all people. You treat the sick, help in the community with your police and prison work, and yet you don't want to support those who've been terrorised and robbed. It's almost as if you're on the side of the criminal.'

His face darkened. 'It would appear you have a short memory. I'll pretend I never heard that. Do I have to tell you again why I don't want you getting involved in any more dangerous situations?'

'Yes, tell me,' she cried, as the promise of the night dwindled.

'You *already know*,' he snapped, 'and yet you don't care. It's because I don't want anything to happen to you. You were happy enough for me to be concerned about you when we first met, but as soon as we knew we were in love, you didn't want me fussing over you. Well, you can have it. If you fall into the river I'll wave to you as I go past.'

'I can swim!' she hissed back, and then dredged up a smile as the rest of the guests came back.

'You look good enough to eat,' Jane said as supper was served by the caterers that Blake had hired.

'Don't believe it,' Helena told her dismally. 'I would leave a bitter taste in your mouth. You'll do much better with the goodies before you.'

'Not another quarrel?'

''Fraid so,' Helena told her. 'Ours was an affair that was over before it began. I came with too many loose strings.'

For the rest of the evening she smiled, ate the food, chatted to those who wanted to talk and stayed silent for those who didn't, and while doing all of that managed to avoid Blake, who was keeping his distance too.

'Thank you for coming,' he said gravely when she was leaving.

Having no wish to tell a lie, she refrained from saying it had been a pleasure.

By the time she got home Helena had decided she was going to do what she should have done after she'd lost her father—go back to Australia.

'Are you sure there will be a position if I come back?' she asked Deborah when she returned her call.

'Yes, definitely,' she was told. 'I'll speak to the nursing manager and ask her to get the authorities to confirm it.'

'I'm going back to Australia,' she told Jane the next morning.

'Oh, no!' she exclaimed. 'You're giving up on Dr Pemberton?'

'He's given up on me.'

'I don't believe that. It was as plain as the nose on my face that last night's effort was all on your behalf. I saw you were deep in conversation when we came back to join you. Was it something to do with that?'

Helena nodded.

'Yes. We're involved in a jumble of ethics, priorities and mixed emotions.'

'That's rubbish and you know it!' Jane declared. 'If ever I saw two people who are right for each other, it's you and him.'

'I don't think so,' Helena told her, 'and I'm not going to change my mind. Blake and I have lost each other somewhere along the way and it's time to make a clean break.'

'So that's what you want?'

'Yes.'

'I don't believe you.'

'I'm going to hand in my notice after morning surgery.'

'So you've actually got a job waiting.'

'Yes.'

Jane's round face crumpled.

'I'm going to miss you, Helena. We've been a good team.'

'So that's what the phone call from Australia was about,' Blake said curtly when she caught him alone in the lunch hour. 'What do you expect to achieve by running away?'

'A new life…crime-free. Peace of mind.'

'Huh!' he snorted. 'Crime is everywhere. You'll have to work a month's notice, Helena.'

So that was it, she thought. No asking her to reconsider. Just a bald statement about working out her notice. She wasn't aware that, reeling from the news, Blake was clutching at straws. Anything to keep her there for as long as possible.

'The practice nurse before me only worked a week's notice,' she pointed out.

'That was domestic. Her move wasn't career connected,' he said quickly.

'And that makes a difference? All right, Blake, I'll work the month out. Are there any other stipulations you want to make?'

She was hoping he would say, 'Yes, you're not going,' but he didn't. He just walked to the door and held it open for her to depart.

When she'd gone he went to stand by the window. So it was over. He squared his shoulders. Not if he could help it. But would it be fair to Helena if he tried to make her change her mind? She'd thought of going back in those first days after her father had died and now was probably wishing she had.

Maybe he'd made himself too indispensable at that time, but as long as he lived he would never forget her face on the morning when she'd opened the door to him, afraid that he'd meant her harm. After that he had been committed to protecting her and nothing had changed, except that his concern had become a deep, abiding love.

There'd been no joy in the day, Helena thought as she returned to the cottage that evening. The moment she'd told Blake she was leaving she'd known she didn't want to go, and if he'd shown the slightest sign of distress or sadness she would have thrown herself into his arms and told him she didn't mean it.

But he hadn't. He'd just harped on about how much notice she was going to have to work and that had been it, with a few sarcastic comments thrown in.

On impulse she got changed and made her way to the Swan, intending to eat there as she couldn't be bothered to make a meal.

Seated at a table for two by the window, she was picking at her food when a shadow fell across her and she looked up to find Blake standing there.

'Am I allowed to join you?' he asked with an ironic lift of the eyebrow.

'Of course,' she said stiffly. 'Though I wasn't expecting to see you here.'

'I would imagine it's for the same reason as yourself. I couldn't work up the enthusiasm to cook. So tell me about the new job,' he said easily, when the waitress had taken his order. 'Where is it and what will you be doing?'

Helena eyed him doubtfully. There seemed to be a change of climate from earlier in the day.

'It will be general nursing in Sydney.'

'Sounds good.'

'Yes. It will be,'

This was ghastly, she was thinking. Polite small talk when just the sight of him made her melt.

'Can't we talk about something other than work?' she asked.

Again there was the raised eyebrow.

'Such as?'

'Whether you've made any further decisions about the house since last night.'

'Ah, yes, the house. Nothing definite yet, but you'll be the first to know.'

'Me!' she said, knocking her wineglass over in the confusion.

Blake got to his feet and went round to help her mop up the red tide that was dripping off the table onto her skirt. His hand brushed against her leg and she froze. It was the slightest of touches but it set her on fire, and as she looked up at him she saw that she wasn't the only one to be affected by the contact.

It was their undoing.

'Let's go,' he said.

'Where to?'

'Does it matter? I can't make love to you in here.'

He put some notes on the table and took her hand, and as the surprised waitress arrived with his meal they went.

'Not the house,' she said when they got outside. 'It wouldn't seem right.'

He flashed her a smile.

'Don't spoil the moment, Helena. The way we feel now it would be right anywhere. We'll go to the cottage, shall we?'

'Mmm,' she said dreamily as they pointed themselves in that direction.

His phone rang as she was putting the key in the lock and he groaned.

'I'm on duty tonight. Please, don't let it be the police.'

As he listened to the voice at the other end his face was grim.

'So when did this happen?' he asked, and after listening to further dialogue he added, 'I'm coming right over. Have you sent for an ambulance? Good. I'll be with you in minutes.'

His face was haggard in the light of the streetlamps as he put the phone back in his pocket.

'*Was* it the police?' Helena asked.

He shook his head.

'No. It's Rowena. She's had a heart attack. Sounds serious. It was the home. They've sent for an ambulance. I have to go, Helena. That woman means the world to me. She has been my salvation.'

'I know,' she said gently, 'as you were hers.' And with eyes misting and blood cooling she went on, 'Go to her, Blake.' As he hesitated, she gave him a gentle push.

He eyed her for a moment and Helena knew she wasn't the only one whose blood had cooled. Blake's probably more so after what he'd just been told.

'Maybe it's not meant to be,' he said wryly, and her heart twisted.

'Maybe,' she agreed tonelessly. 'It was a spur-of-the-moment thing anyway, wasn't it?'

He nodded and as he turned to go for his car, still in the hotel car park, she wondered just how disappointed he was that their love-making hadn't materialised.

She hadn't offered to go with him, sensing that he would want to be alone with the woman who meant so much to him, but she called after him, 'You'll let me know what's happening, won't you?'

'Yes,' he replied sombrely, and with eyes troubled and spirits at zero she went inside and closed the door.

Later, as she lay sleepless between the sheets, Helena thought that she would be glad when this day was over. There'd been the handing in of her notice and Blake's cold re-action, followed by her sudden decision to dine out and his unexpected appearance. Then the spilling of the wine had been responsible for desire kindling between them. Desire that had gone unsated after the phone call about Rowena.

Where was Blake now? she wondered. By her bedside in some shadowed ward. Praying that she wouldn't be taken from him.

CHAPTER TEN

IT WAS four o'clock in the morning when the doorbell rang and roused Helena from a restless doze.

Blake, she thought as she sped down the stairs. He was back. It hadn't occurred to her that it would be anyone else, but with her hand on the door catch she called his name.

'Yes, it's me,' he said.

His face looked grey and drawn in the dim light as she opened up for him, and as he stepped inside she found she was holding her breath.

'She's dead, Helena,' he said woodenly. 'Rowena is dead. She'd gone before I got there. I never had the chance to say goodbye. When the ambulance came they tried to resuscitate her but it was too late.'

'Oh, no!' she breathed. 'And she never saw you move into her house.'

'Don't remind me,' he said. 'It was all over in minutes, according to the staff at the home, and, of course, that's how she would have wanted it to be. No lingering and lack of dignity. But I shall miss her so.'

She wanted to take him in her arms and soothe away his grief, but grief, as she had cause to know, was not so easily soothed away.

'I'll make you a cup of tea,' she said, feeling that as gestures went it was inadequate to say the least.

He shook his head. 'No. I'll go home. I'm sorry I've dragged you out of bed, but as you'd met her I thought you'd like to know.'

'I can't let you go home,' she said gently, 'not like this. It can be *your* turn to sleep in *my* spare room.' As he opened his mouth to protest, she said, 'Don't argue, Blake. You didn't leave me alone when I lost my father and I'm not leaving you alone now.'

He gave a tired smile. 'All right, but I can't see myself doing much sleeping.'

'You have to. There will be much for you to do tomorrow and with sleep comes escape from the sorrow.'

He did sleep. Helena left it an hour and then crept into the spare room to check on him. He was lying on his side with his face all crunched up, and as she looked down at him she knew once and for all where she belonged.

Gently she eased herself onto the bed behind him, curling up against his back so carefully that he never moved. Then her arms went round him and as he groaned in his sleep she pressed her lips against his broad back.

They'd ended up sleeping together after all, she thought, but not in passion. It was a different sort of need that had brought her to his bed. Blake's need. For once he wasn't the strong one. Grief-stricken and desolate, he'd come to her, and that was something she wasn't going to forget.

As she felt the strong, regular beat of his heart beneath her hand she knew that there were dark days ahead for him. She'd been there. Knew the score. And if he would let her, she would help him through them.

When she awoke in a wintry dawn he'd gone, leaving only the imprint of his head on the pillow to say that he'd been there. When she reached out to touch the place where he'd lain it was still warm, and she swung herself out of the bed. Maybe he was downstairs, making a drink, or in the bathroom, but she was too late. He'd gone and she wouldn't know until she saw him again what he'd thought of her sharing his bed.

To her amazement he was at the practice when she got there. He'd obviously been home, shaved and changed the clothes that he'd slept in. The grief-stricken man of the night before had been replaced by the brisk GP. Only she knew what it must have cost him to put his desolation on hold for the sake of his patients.

'How are you?' she asked quietly, thinking that now he would say something about finding her beside him.

He gave a bleak smile. 'Adjusting to the unalterable,' he said flatly. 'And what about you?'

'What about me?'

'I barged in on you at some ungodly hour.'

'And you think I wouldn't have wanted you to?'

'Maybe.'

'Then you're wrong.'

'I seem to be wrong about a lot of things these days.'

Surely now he was going to mention her lying next to him in the night, but it seemed not.

'I have a funeral to arrange,' he said. 'Will you come?'

'Me?'

'Yes. You. Rowena liked you.'

'Of course I'll come if you want me to. Just as long as her family won't feel I'm in the way.'

'She had no family. There will be just you and I and Mrs Porteous. Some of the neighbouring bigwigs will probably turn up to pay their respects, but in the actual funeral party there will just be we three.'

It was obviously going to be a very quiet affair, she thought, and then had to change her mind when he went on to say, 'I shall see to it that food is laid on at the house for anyone who wants to join us afterwards.'

'Yes. I see,' she said slowly, having to accept that as far as Blake was concerned what had happened—or not happened—between the two of them the night before had been swept under the carpet, and it was hardly the right moment to drag it back into the light of day.

When he'd awakened to find the sweet warmth of Helena curved against his back, Blake hadn't wanted to move. He'd known her presence there had been completely sexless. Helena had wanted to comfort him and she couldn't have chosen a better way.

He'd wanted to stay there for ever with her breasts up against his shoulder blades and her breath gently fanning his neck, but he'd had to face the day ahead. His sorrow at having lost Rowena had been like a leaden weight around his heart, but there had been the practice to attend to, the undertaker to see, Mrs Porteous to be told the sad news, and he could imagine the state she would be in. She'd been Rowena's housekeeper for many years.

With a sigh he'd eased himself carefully off the bed and stood looking down at Helena. He hadn't got the monopoly on loving care, he'd thought wryly. He'd been wrong to assume that it was all on one side. She'd been there for him during the night, and it was a thought that would warm him every time he felt the chill that came with death. It would also be something to hold onto if she kept to her resolve to go back to Australia.

And as he'd shut the bedroom door quietly behind him and crept down the stairs, he'd known that if she went it would be as if he'd been twice bereaved.

Before the funeral there was a service in the big parish church where Rowena had worshipped all her life, and as Helena sat between Blake and a tearful Mrs Porteous she was reminded of how near Christmas was. The crib was in place before the altar and a large spruce stood beneath a glowing stained-glass window.

At a time of great rejoicing the man beside her was going to be filled with sadness, she thought. And what about her? If she kept to her plans she would be flying to Australia some time during the Christmas holidays, as by then she would have worked out her notice.

There was a snag, though. She'd never written back to confirm the official job offer that she'd received. The letter was there, waiting to be posted, but every time she thought about doing it she put it off.

Blake had never mentioned it since that night in the Swan, so she was taking it that he'd accepted her decision and was just going to let her go. She knew that he'd had a lot on his mind of recent days and her affairs would have been shelved.

Quite a few people did come to the house after the funeral was over and Helena thought that she was here again...as a visitor... and any patter of tiny feet in time to come wouldn't belong to her children.

This time, though, visitor or not, she was doing the honours with Blake, standing beside him as he welcomed those who'd come to pay their respects, and if she was the object of a few curious glances, what did she care?

When they'd gone he said, 'Now that I've laid Rowena to rest, I'll be able to give some attention to other things.'

'Such as?'

'Your departure, the new partner at the practice and Christmas, just to mention a few.'

She noticed that her leaving had been listed along with other items. It hadn't been mentioned as something particularly important and suddenly aggravated she said, 'You don't need to concern yourself about my affairs. The Australia business is all signed and sealed.'

'I see. So what date are you planning on leaving?'

'Christmas Eve,' she said perversely, having no intention of doing any such thing. She couldn't leave him alone for two reasons. It would be their first Christmas—and probably the last—and he'd just lost Rowena.

But having made the announcement, he would be expecting her to keep to it, no matter how unfeeling he thought her, and she wished she hadn't been so quick off the mark.

'I'll drive you home,' he said, as if they'd been discussing trivialities.

'No. I'll walk.'

'Suit yourself, but one thing before you go. Now that I have time to gather my wits, I'd like to buy you a farewell gift. We've seen a lot of each other over these last months and I can't let you go without something for you to remember it by.'

She wanted to yell at him, 'I'll have an aching heart to remember it by. Do you have to keep turning the screw by letting me see how relaxed you are at the thought of seeing the back of me?'

Instead, she told him, 'I've been thinking of doing the same for you.'

'So we'll go shopping together soon.'

Was he crazy? she thought. Or just thick-skinned, suggesting they go shopping for farewell gifts when her heart was breaking?

They'd had an affair of sorts and now it was over. He'd just laid Rowena to rest and seemed as if he was ready to do the same with that.

'I'll pick you up on Saturday afternoon if that's all right with you,' he was saying, and she found herself nodding like an obedient puppet.

*   *   *

When Jane heard what they were planning she rolled her eyes heavenwards and said, 'What are you two like!'

'Don't ask me,' Helena replied. 'It was Blake's idea.'

'So you really are leaving…and he doesn't mind?'

'That seems to be the case.'

'Have you ever slept together?' she asked.

Helena smiled, her mouth soft and tender.

'Yes.'

'What was it like?'

'The ultimate in togetherness.'

'And yet you're letting each other go.'

'Yes.'

'What did you actually quarrel about in the first place?'

'Stupid things. Pride and prejudice.'

'That doesn't sound like either of you.'

'No. It *was* more than that. I got caught up in a robbery at a jeweller's and I came face to face with the only one of the thieves who wasn't masked. The police asked me if I would be a witness if they caught them. I said I would and Blake went ballistic.'

'Well, he would, wouldn't he?' Jane said in slow surprise. 'We all know what happens to people who do the right thing and then wish they hadn't. They can be on the move for the rest of their lives.'

She had never told anyone about her father's predicament and she wasn't going to now, but Helena wondered what Jane would say if she knew just how close she herself had been to that sort of situation.

'I wanted to do the right thing, but he didn't or wouldn't understand. So far nothing has come of it, so it looks as if we quarrelled about a hypothetical situation.'

'But he loves you, for heaven's sake, and he's a police surgeon. He's involved in the crime scene more than most people. He would know better than anyone the danger you were exposing yourself to,' Jane protested. 'He's already lost one woman he loved because of the stupidity of others. Surely you understand that.'

'Yes, I do. But there's more to it than that.'

There was. The Kelsall brothers riding roughshod over decent law-abiding people for one thing, the poor woman in the hotel grounds and her father driven from the family home.

Where it would have traumatised most people, in her case, afraid though she was, it had had the opposite effect. It had brought out her fighting instincts and she'd become embattled with Blake in the process.

There was no easy answer, but talking to Jane had helped to clear her mind. By concerning herself about others she'd shown no consideration for the feelings of the man who'd put *her* safety above all else.

As the patients came and went during the day Jane's comments kept coming back to mind. Her friend was right, she thought. Blake and herself were wasting precious time by getting their priorities wrong, and she was going to do something about it at the first opportunity.

There was just one patient waiting outside the nurses' room as the day drew to a close, and when Helena glanced at her notes before calling her in, her eyes widened. The address was that of the neat detached house where she'd found her father living when she'd come back from Australia. She was about to meet the bank manager's wife. The woman who'd been having panic attacks was here with a badly sprained ankle. She'd seen Darren and he'd passed her on to the practice nurses to have it strapped up.

'I'm a walking disaster at the moment,' Jean McIntosh said when she came limping in. 'I think it's because I'm not being as careful as I should. Too much on my mind. We've only recently moved to these parts. There has been so much to do, so many changes in a very short time.'

Helena flashed her a sympathetic smile. 'I haven't been living here long myself so I know the feeling. It takes time to adjust. You are Dr Pemberton's new neighbour, aren't you?'

'Yes, that's right. Do you know the area?'

Did she know the area!

'Yes. I know it very well,' she said, and could have added 'to my cost.'

'It's only for a short time,' Jean was saying. 'We're having a house built but it isn't ready yet. One of the other neighbours was saying that the place we're renting is like a transit camp. No one seems to stay there long.'

When she'd gone Helena sank down onto the nearest chair. The past kept sending out its reminders. Her father had been a previous occupier and there'd been a very good reason why his stay had been short. But it was strange. After talking to the bank manager's wife she felt as if that part of the past had cleansed itself.

There was an ordinary family living in the house now, and their only problems were those felt by anyone having to get used to new surroundings. The shadow of the witness protection programme had been lifted and with it a dark chapter of her life. It had been the past that had been blighting her relationship with Blake. Was she going to let herself become involved in another situation that brought danger with it?

Ever since Rowena's funeral Blake had kept remembering Helena standing beside him as they'd greeted the mourners. It had felt so right to have her there. It was where she belonged.

To even think of letting her go to Australia was beyond belief.

It had been Rowena's dearest wish that his children should be brought up in the house, and that wasn't going to happen unless he did something about it. As he'd eaten his solitary evening meal the resolve had been strengthening in him and, he knew that the first thing he had to do was admit that he'd been wrong, wrong in insisting that Helena was not to help the police.

He'd let his love for her override his integrity and in doing so had tainted the precious thing that had become the mainspring of his life.

The time for misunderstandings was past. Whether Helena went away or not, he had to tell her that she'd been right. That evil must not be allowed to flourish.

Mrs Porteous opened the door to Helena's ring on the bell and, breathing hard with the tenseness of the moment, she asked, 'Is Blake in?'

'He went out not ten minutes ago, my dear,' the housekeeper told her.

'Do you know where he went, Mrs Porteous?' she asked.

'I'm afraid I don't. He usually says but not this time. He seemed to be in a hurry. Would you like to come in and wait?'

'Er…no, thanks,' she said deflatedly. 'Maybe I'll call back later.'

As she pointed the car in the direction of the cottage, she thought that it was typical. She'd shilly-shallied around for weeks and the moment she'd decided to do something about it, he wasn't there.

The lights were on but there was no answer. On another occasion Blake would have left, but not tonight. The feeling of urgency in him was so strong he was going to stay on the doorstep until Helena came back, no matter what the hour.

He didn't have to wait long. When her car pulled up beside his he was out of the driver's seat in a flash and so was she. As the moment took hold of them he said, 'I've come to tell you that you were right, Helena, and I was wrong. I got my values mixed up. Can you forgive me?'

He saw her mouth curve into softness.

'There's nothing to forgive, Blake. That's where I've been. To your place, to tell you that *you* were right and *I* was wrong and that we're never going to let the past come between us again. Jane made me see what a selfish beast I've been and this afternoon I talked to the woman who lives next door to you and she made me see things in a different light, too. I don't know whether you still want me, but I had to put things right between us.'

'Want you!' he breathed. 'I ache for you.'

'Yet you were going to let me go to Australia.'

'Oh, no, I wasn't. My farewell gift to you was going to be a ring that I was going to put on the third finger of your left hand even if I had to hold you down while I did it. And if that didn't make you change your mind I was going to kidnap you from the airport.'

They weren't even touching, but it was as if they were blended into one as she told him

laughingly, 'You might have found that difficult.'

'Why?'

'Because I'm not going. Never was. My letter of acceptance was never posted. And,
Blake...'

'Yes?'

'Once you touch me my thinking processes
will cease to function, so can I ask it now?
You've never said what you thought when you
found me in your bed.'

His mouth was tender. 'Some things are too
precious to talk about. I was hoping the memory of it would get me through the bad days
ahead.'

'So you didn't mind?'

'Mind!' he echoed in mock astonishment. 'It
was the reason I admitted to being wrong. So
that I could awake each morning with you beside me for the rest of my life.'

'So does that mean you want me to marry
you?'

'It seems to be the best way to fill the house
with the children that Rowena wanted to see
there.'

'Maybe one day we'll have daughter,' she said softly.

'With russet locks and green eyes,' he added.

'And we'll call her Rowena.'

'Absolutely,' he agreed.

A cough from nearby broke into the moment and they stared as a police constable approached.

'It's Dr Pemberton, isn't it?' he said. 'I've seen you at the station, but it's the lady I've come to see.'

'Me?' Helena questioned warily.

'Yes, madam. The doctor was asking if we'd caught the gang who did the robbery at the town centre jeweller's a couple of months back. At the time we hadn't, but we were hot on their trail and the sergeant sent me round to tell you that we've got them and there won't be any need for you to be involved as they've all admitted it.'

'Thank you, Constable,' she said gravely. 'I appreciate you taking the trouble to come and tell me.'

'Think nothing of it,' he said with a grin. 'It's all part of the service.'

When he'd gone Blake smiled. 'What timing! If he'd come any earlier he might have confused the issue.'

'I don't think so,' she said with an answering beam. 'We both knew who was wrong and who was right, didn't we?'

'Did we?' he asked teasingly as he took her into his arms, and then it was as she'd said it would be, thinking processes out of order, sweet chemistry clocking in.

They'd bought the ring. Blake had put it on the finger where it belonged and she'd reminded him smilingly, 'So, you see, you didn't have to use force after all.'

'No indeed,' he'd agreed gravely as he'd looked down at the circlet of sapphires and diamonds. 'But I won't believe that you're really mine until I see a gold band next to it.'

They were walking through the gardens of the house and frost lay upon the trees in silver fronds.

'You will,' she promised.

'Yes, but when? A big wedding can take months to arrange.'

'So let's have a small one.'

He shook his head. 'No. This place will be perfect for a big winter wedding. We'll just have to speed things up.'

'And you're thinking that it's what Rowena would have wanted, aren't you?' she asked softly.

'Yes, I am. Do you mind?'

'Of course not. How could I? If it hadn't been for her we would never have had the chance to live in such a place. We're so lucky to have each other and all this.'

'I'm going to give up my extra commitments,' he told her.

'What? Your police surgeon work and the prison contract?'

'Yes. I think we've seen enough of that sort of thing.'

Helena shook her head. 'Don't do that, Blake. The people you come across in those situations need someone like you who is fair and unbiased. Don't forget that I was once one of your waifs and strays.'

He laughed. 'There's not all that much difference between waif and wife, is there?'

The daffodils were out and the heady scent of hyacinths hung on the air as the wedding car pulled up outside the church. Bells were pealing high above and inside the bridegroom waited for his bride.

Mrs Porteous was there, sporting a new hat, and behind her were the staff from the practice and other friends.

There'd been no male relative to walk her down the aisle and to Jane's delight Helena had asked her to give her away and now they were there, poised ready in the open doorway.

Out of the corner of her eye Helena saw Jean McIntosh in the back pew and they exchanged smiles. They'd spoken a few times since the day she'd sprained her ankle and it had made such a difference to Jean, finding a new friend.

The organ was striking up. Those present were getting to their feet and Helena thought joyfully, Blake was there, waiting to make her his wife...

MEDICAL ROMANCE™

Large Print

Titles for the next six months...

November

THE DOCTOR'S UNEXPECTED FAMILY	Lilian Darcy
HIS PREGNANT GP	Lucy Clark
THE ENGLISH DOCTOR'S BABY	Sarah Morgan
THE SURGEON'S SECRET SON	Rebecca Lang

December

IN DR DARLING'S CARE	Marion Lennox
A COURAGEOUS DOCTOR	Alison Roberts
THE BABY RESCUE	Jessica Matthews
THE CONSULTANT'S ACCIDENTAL BRIDE	Carol Marinelli

January

LIKE DOCTOR, LIKE SON	Josie Metcalfe
THE A&E CONSULTANT'S SECRET	Lilian Darcy
THE DOCTOR'S SPECIAL CHARM	Laura MacDonald
THE SPANISH CONSULTANT'S BABY	Kate Hardy

MILLS & BOON®

Live the emotion

1004 LP 2P P1 Medical

MEDICAL ROMANCE™

Large Print

MILLS & BOON®

Live the emotion

1004 LP 2P P2 Medical